Bowyer Nichols

Words and Days

A Table-Book of Prose and Verse

Bowyer Nichols

Words and Days
A Table-Book of Prose and Verse

ISBN/EAN: 9783337366797

Printed in Europe, USA, Canada, Australia, Japan

Cover: Foto ©Andreas Hilbeck / pixelio.de

More available books at **www.hansebooks.com**

WORDS AND DAYS

A TABLE-BOOK OF PROSE AND VERSE

COMPILED BY

BOWYER NICHOLS

WITH AN INTRODUCTION BY

GEORGE SAINTSBURY

LONDON
RIVINGTON, PERCIVAL AND CO.
1895

INTRODUCTION

THE best excuse that I can find for interposing myself, even by invitation, between the reader and the book that follows, is that the contriver of it could not with equal decency affirm his enjoyment of his handiwork. I have read these portions, or selections, or whatever it may be decided to call them, with a pleasure not materially dashed, and perhaps I might say materially heightened, by observing the number of things contained therein which are favourites of my own, but which I had not thought likely to be fixed upon by anybody else. This is a sentiment which, if it comes in a certain egotistic satisfaction short of, certainly exceeds in true liberality, the more usual reflection on anthologies of any kind—'Why has this man omitted what I think the best things?'

I do not know that the general plan of the book needs any defence, except perhaps to those *jeunes féroces* who are angry at the antiquated attractions of the Past being put forward as rivals to the Present, and more angry still at any present lovers of these elder beauties assuming the office of heralds and harbingers thereto. Even they might be softened by the commixture of old and new here, which must be admitted to be arranged on no grudging scale as regards contemporaries.

To me this mixture of old and new is one, if not the chief, of the attractions of the book. To find, in something more than a fortuitous conjunction, texts from Mallory and Mr. Morris, Raleigh and Omar Khayyám (or rather FitzGerald), Mr. Meredith and Daniel, Vaughan and Carlyle, Chaucer and Mr. Ruskin, has for the lover of literature who knows that in literature time does not exist, a relish not easily equalled by any collection of things new only or only old. I cannot imagine a more excellent way of knocking down with a double swashing-blow the two most pestilent errors of all literary appreciation—the notion of Progress and the notion of Decadence—than this ingenious juxtaposition: and I hope that the due meditation of this little book may convince at any rate some readers of the ugly and fallacious nature of these two giants. South may have put the thing sweepingly when he said that 'an Aristotle was but the rubbish of an Adam'; but perhaps we may make a not much less great mistake if we assert that an Aristotle was but the rudiments of a Darwin.

I have said 'the due meditation,' and indeed nobody who reads far will fail to see that this collection is no mere commonplace-book, no bundle of elegant extracts. The constructor of it has endeavoured, and I think very successfully endeavoured, to secure unity now of thought, now of subject, now of allusion, now of all three, in his portions. He has done more; he has secured a not inconsiderable connection between the various selections for the same month, and between these selections and the conventional character of the month itself, so that if the Publishers care to issue a quarto edition with elaborate allegorical illustrations, they will not have much difficulty in prescribing subjects to their artist. But the diurnal unity is greater, as it should be. Having read the book with no illegitimate or private information as to the author's objects, I may possibly be putting into his head thoughts that he did not think; but I should be slow to be convinced of this. The more obvious suggestions, such as that of the pieces for January 26, the anniversary of the Fall of Khartoum, as those of Saint Valentine and All Fools' Day and May Day, will of course strike everybody: unfortunately, I fear that Saint Valentine now requires such a flapper or reminder of him. I note a delicate conceit in the selections for April 19, wherein, by the juxtaposition of the famous Primrose-salad passage, and the still more famous one from *Peter Bell*, it is made obvious that a man who sees in a primrose the potentiality of salad is of a far higher order of development than is he who sees in it nothing but a primrose. From which we may go far.

But these things are mere *secrets de Polichinelle*—everybody can find them out. The keynote of the triads is not always so clear-sounding, and though I believe it is always to be found, it does not always obtrude itself. In some of the juxtapositions I think there will be found an agreeable unexpectedness, and in most a pleasing congruity. It is good to have, put side by side, the poetical idealism and the sober (but sober is not the word) fact of Lovelace's famous prison song, and of the actual performance, at very nearly the same time, of Lady Fanshawe, when she stole with the dark lantern at four o'clock in the morning under the prison windows, and the rain drenched her from head to foot. More quaint and subjective, but not less agreeable, is the combination of Miss Podsnap and Delilah as exhibiting various aspects of the Woman of

Philistia. I am not sorry to see a few extracts in which there may be a little puzzlement for those who only know literature by handbooks. For instance, in Addison's passage about the Black Prince and the Emperor of Germany, the exact appropriateness (and it is very exact) to its sister passages may not strike those who do not know the context. From this, in generous minds, comes that hunting up of the context which is the only certain highway to real literary knowledge. And I am also glad to see that Mr. Nichols has included not a few things from quite modern books which have had their day of popularity and have been unjustly forgotten, or which, having their day of popularity now, are likely to be forgotten soon. Such a piece, for instance, as the few lines from one of those scenes in which Anthony Trollope approached, if he did not reach, supremacy—the finale of the flirtation with Madalina Demolines—is at once an act of redress and a warning. Few selectors, I think, have been so hardy as to dare to place the assured and unquestionable, because tried and proved, treasures of the past beside the dusty and problematical remains of yesterday, and the still more problematical, if not so dusty, products of the day. That none may presume Mr. Nichols has given Raleigh's 'Death' passage, and the 'Lion and the Leopard,' and Landor's fatal contrast of reputation and fame; that none may despair he has given such things as that just quoted, and plentiful extracts from the modernest of the modern.

If, however, there should still be (and I have often seen it expressed lately) a prejudice against 'scraps,' against 'beauties,' and so forth, a few words may not be amiss as an endeavour to show cause against it. There is something rather plausible, rather apparently generous, in such a prejudice; most of us, I suppose, can remember a time when we shared it. It has a touch of nobility to say, 'Thank you; I do not want shreds and patches; I will have the whole; I will read and select for myself.' But perhaps the answer, 'Yes; but *do* you?' is a little uncomfortable, a little damaging. It is sometimes said that nowadays we read too little; I should rather say that we read too much and too rapidly. It is a commonplace that an ordinary daily newspaper contains the matter of a fair-sized octavo volume; and an ordinary weekly newspaper contains about the same or a little less. So that, if a man reads only one of each, he reads an octavo volume every day throughout the year, or about ten thousand volumes in thirty years, quite independently of all other reading. A most respectable total! But what does he read, and how does he read it? Certainly not to mark, learn, and inwardly digest, which perhaps is in the circumstances all the better for him. Even in reading books, whether new or old, which *are* books, how many people take more than passing note, if they take note at all, of the 'jewels five words long,' when there are such jewels? Private commonplace books have almost gone out—a disuse which perhaps has its good side as well as its bad. The habit of quotation has gone out very much likewise, which undoubtedly has its good side as well as its bad. But the disuse of both for the custom of rapid, careless reading can hardly be thought to have been without evil effects. It is a trite maxim that failure to exercise the faculty of attention leads to the same result as in the case of any other faculty; and though this result may be convenient to the rapid writer, it can hardly be thought to be entirely without inconvenience to the rapid reader. It is possible to have a too quick as well as a too slow digestion.

Now with books of this kind, which have been in fashion in times at least as good as ours, and which may be in fashion again, there is no need, and comparatively little temptation, to read rapidly, and there is every opportunity to read with reflection. I do not know how many readers will be obedient to the actual scheme, and read their portion, and not more than their portion, daily. It is not an obedient age, except when it is told to do something foolish, when it usually 'goes and does it' with an exactitude which would have left Mr. Squeers himself with very little excuse for inflicting chastisement. But even in mere turning over, the shortness of the texts must give them an additional chance of being remembered. And having myself turned them over and something more, I should say that they are for the most part rememberable and meditable with a great deal of advantage and satisfaction. Mr. Nichols has certainly not proceeded on that principle of Selden's which he has put on the forefront of his book, and which would have met, and no doubt did meet, with much hearty approval from Dr. Folliott. Not that I think there are many 'scullions in the kitchen' here; but I suspect Selden would have thought so, and so, perhaps, would his friend Ben, who, nevertheless, provided as notable and quotable things as most ancients can boast. The truth is, that the late sixteenth and early seventeenth century carried to extremity, and indeed to caricature, that preference for the ancient over the modern which in certain other times, not necessary to specify, has toppled over by the usual sequence, and turned into an equally extravagant and caricatured preference for the modern over the ancient. Here, as I have already hinted, nobody can find fault with either the one or the other excess.

I dare say the invariable precedence of a Shakesperean citation will annoy some people; but I am afraid they are the people whom it is right and proper to annoy. But no one, I think, can justly urge a too great preponderance of any single author in the citations which come second and third; and most fair judges will admit an unusual and creditable catholicity which has not even feared to take from living authors, though the exclusion of these, whether it be a counsel of perfection or not, is certainly a counsel of discretion. Some of these living authors, as well as some more or less recently dead, have probably suffered in most people's minds that peril of rapid reading which has been referred to, and the public might, until confronted with the quotations, say in their haste, as Dr. Folliott in his said of Scott, that their works contain nothing quotable. It will have been a good deed to demonstrate the error.

Even from the most careless reading there should come pleasure and profit,—a sort of pleasure and profit which only an olio, only a medley can give. It is right pleasant to pass from Campion's rose-cheeked Laura to Carlyle's gigantic Hat; from that anecdote of More's concerning the persecuted member of the congregation who retaliated on the preacher (a crime which, I fear, we have all of us many times longed to commit) to George Herbert's grave deprecation of such conduct immediately afterwards. Here shall you find the verb to 'haberdash,' which I remember a too rigid editor cutting as 'not English' out of an article of mine, though I asked him in the most persuasive manner whether he thought 'haberdasher' was a Melchizedek among words and had no verb-parent. Here you may on two consecutive pages observe and compare two different examples of irony by Miss Austen and Matthew Arnold, on which homilies—volumes—might be composed not superfluously. One passage, a passage from Thackeray, will suggest the amazing, the incomparable duncery of those wiseacres who call Thackeray a cynic; and another from Sir John Davies may set you wondering how that exceedingly clever lawyer and poet managed, all but three hundred years ago, to write exactly as if he had been writing three hundred years later. Here one catches oneself falling in love again (for to read her is to love her) with Dorothy Osborne, and there chuckling with Bishop Earle over his 'gallant,' who 'gratulated the first sin, and the fig leaves that were an occasion for bravery.'

One of the uses of the book that, not knowing of its aim thereat, I was most pleased at discovering, is its performance of the function of a birthday-book, not in the vulgar sense, but in that of a calendar, recording by appropriate entries the birthdays of great men, and especially poets. As a rule the Englishman is but a sparing and infrequent observer of days. It was remarked not long ago in the House of Commons, I think, with not unjustifiable sarcasm, when a certain very unwise officer had meddled with the celebration of St. Patrick's Day, or St. David's, that probably he himself could not have told St. George's Day if he had been asked. And, by the way, I would Mr. Nichols had celebrated St. George as well as St. William on the twenty-third of April. This laches of ours is no small pity; for every commemoration of the past, every linking of the common dying things that are, with the immortal and stable things that have been, is an infinite gain for the health and the life, the pleasure and the profit of the soul. Nor, perhaps, is the least or least welcome feature of this little book to be found in the fact that, in more ways than one or two, it thus vivifies the course of time, which is apt to be so little vivid, and diversifies by the suggestion of worthy memories and interests the monotony of existence. Mr. Stevenson, not, I think, with all his usual insight, once noted it as a piece of childishness in Pepys that he was constantly saying to himself, 'Don't you remember.' If it was, it was a survival of childhood which some of the best and some of the most fortunate of men have carried furthest into middle life and age. And it is not only personal memories which may do us this good turn, but memories literary, historical, memories of all kinds. To the task of fixing their commemorations Mr. Nichols has given some help in this book, and he deserves no little thanks for having done so.

GEORGE SAINTSBURY.

Weeds among weeds; or flowers with flowers gather'd.

SONN. CXIV.

JANUARY

My library were dukedom large enough.

TEMPEST i. 2.

IN quoting of books quote such authors as are usually read; others you may read for your own satisfaction, but not to name them.

To quote a modern Dutchman, where you may use a classic author, is as if I were to justify my reputation, and neglect all persons of note and quality that know me, and bring the testimonial of the scullion in the kitchen.

SELDEN.

But ask not, to what doctors I apply?
Sworn to no master, of no sect am I:
As drives the storm, at any door I knock:
And house with Montaigne now, or now
with Locke.

POPE.

In the reproof of chance
Lies the true proof of men.

TROIL. AND CRESS. i. 3.

HEAVEN prepares good men with crosses; but no ill can happen to a good man. . . . That which happens to any man, may to every man. But it is in his reason what he accounts it and will make it.

BEN JONSON.

GIVE me a spirit that on life's rough sea
Loves to have his sails fill'd with a lusty wind,
Even till his sail-yards tremble, his masts crack,
And his rapt ship run on her side so low
That she drinks water, and her keel ploughs air.
There is no danger to a man that knows
What life and death is; there 's not any law
Exceeds his knowledge; neither is it lawful
That he should stoop to any other law.

CHAPMAN.

Who tells me truth, though in his tale lie death,
I hear him as he flattered.

ANT. AND CLEOP. i. 2.

THEY are the troublers, they are the dividers of unity, who neglect and permit not others to unite the dissevered pieces which are yet wanting to the body of truth. To be still searching what we know not, by what we know, still closing up truth to truth as we find it (for all her body is homogeneal and proportional), this is the golden rule.

MILTON.

OUR souls, whose faculties can comprehend
The wondrous architecture of the world,
And measure every wandering planet's course,
Still climbing after knowledge infinite,
And always moving with the restless spheres,
Wills us to wear ourselves and never rest
Until we reach the ripest fruit of all.

MARLOWE.

That my most jealous and too doubtful soul
May live at peace.

TWELFTH NIGHT iv. 3.

I WILL not enter into the question, how much truth is preferable to peace. Perhaps truth may be far better. But as we have scarcely ever the same certainty in the one that we have in the other, I would, unless the truth were evident indeed, hold fast to peace.

BURKE.

FOR this, the wisest of all moral men
Said, 'He knew naught, but that he naught did
know,'
And the great Mocking-Master mocked not then
When he said, 'Truth was buried deep below.'

For why should we the busy soul believe,
When boldly she concludes of that or this;
When of her self she can no judgment give,
Nor how, nor whence, nor where, nor what she is?

SIR JOHN DAVIES.

Subtle as Sphinx: as sweet and musical
As bright Apollo's lute, strung with his hair.

LOVE'S LABOUR'S LOST iv. 3.

SURE there is music even in the beauty and the silent note which Cupid strikes, far sweeter than the sound of an instrument.

SIR THOMAS BROWNE.

ROSE-CHEEKED Laura, come!
Sing thou smoothly with thy beauty's
Silent music, either other
Sweetly gracing.

Lovely forms do flow
From concent divinely framed,
Heaven is music, and thy beauty's
Birth is heavenly.

These dull notes we sing
Discords need for helps to grace them;
Only beauty purely loving
Knows no discord;

But still moves delight,
Like clear springs renewed by flowing,
Ever perfect, ever in them-
Selves eternal.

CAMPION.

What is this,
That rises like the issue of a king,
And wears upon his baby-brow the round
And top of sovereignty?

MACBETH iv. 1.

WHEN they came to Bethlehem, and the star pointed them to a stable, they entered in: and being enlightened with a divine ray, proceeding from the face of the Holy Child, and seeing through the cloud, and passing through the scandal of His mean lodging and poor condition, they bowed themselves to the earth; then they made offering of their gifts, gold, frankincense, and myrrh, protesting their faith of three articles by the symbolical oblation: by gold, that He was a king; by incense, that He was a god; by myrrh, that He was a man.

JEREMY TAYLOR.

SEE how from far, upon the eastern road,
The star-led wizards haste with odours sweet:
O run, prevent them with thy humble ode,
And lay it lowly at His blessed feet;
Have thou the honour first thy Lord to greet,
And join thy voice unto the angel quire,
From out His secret altar touch'd with hallow'd fire.

MILTON.

And such a deal of skimble-skamble stuff
As puts me from my faith.

I KING HENRY IV. iii. I.

IF I durst be bold to tell so sad a man a merry tale, I would tell him of the friar, that as he was preaching in the country, spied a poor wife of the parish whispering with her pew-fellow, and he falling angry thereto, cried out unto her aloud, 'Hold thy babble, I bid thee, thou wife in the red hood.' Which when the housewife heard, she waxed as angry again, and suddenly she start up and cried out unto the friar again, that all the church rang thereon: 'Marry, sir, I beshrew his heart that babbleth most of us both. For I do but whisper a word with my neighbour here, and thou hast babbled there all this hour.'

THOMAS MORE.

JUDGE not the preacher, for he is thy judge:
If thou mislike him, thou conceiv'st him not.
God calleth preaching folly. Do not grudge
To pick out treasures from an earthen pot.
  The worst speak something good: if all want sense,
  God takes a text, and preacheth patience.

GEORGE HERBERT.

Be clamorous, and leap all civil bounds
Rather than make unprofited return.

TWELFTH NIGHT i. 4.

CONSIDER, for example, that great Hat, seven feet high, which now perambulates London Streets: which my Friend Sauerteig regarded justly as one of our English notabilities; 'the topmost point as yet,' said he, 'would it were your culminating and returning point, to which English Puffery has been observed to reach!' The Hatter in the Strand of London, instead of making better felt hats than another, mounts a huge lath-and-plaster Hat, seven feet high, upon wheels; sends a man to drive it through the streets; hoping to be saved thereby.

CARLYLE.

WHAT mean dull souls in this high measure
To haberdash
In earth's base wares, whose greatest treasure
Is dross and trash;
The height of whose enchanting pleasure
Is but a flash?
Are these the goods that thou suppliest
Us mortals with? Are these the highest?
Can these bring cordial peace? False world, thou liest.

QUARLES.

I think good thoughts, while others write good words,
And, like unletter'd clerk, still cry 'Amen.'

SONN. LXXXV.

IN many other points she came on exceedingly well, for though she could not write sonnets she brought herself to read them; and though there seemed no chance of her throwing a whole party into raptures by a prelude on the pianoforte of her own composition, she could listen to other people's performance with very little fatigue.

JANE AUSTEN.

WHAT more felicity can fall to creature
Than to enjoy delight with liberty,
And to be lord of all the works of nature,
To range in th' air from th' earth to highest sky,
To feed on flowers and weeds of glorious feature,
To take whatever thing doth please the eye?
Who rests not pleased with such happiness,
Well worthy he to taste of wretchedness.

SPENSER.

Death, as the Psalmist saith, is certain to all: all shall die. How a good yoke of bullocks at Stamford fair?

2 KING HENRY IV. iii. 2.

'SUPPOSE the worst to happen,' I said, addressing a portly jeweller from Cheapside; 'suppose even yourself to be the victim; *il n'y a pas d'homme nécessaire.* We should miss you for a day or two upon the Woodford branch: but the great mundane movement would still go on, the gravel walks of your villa would still be rolled, dividends would still be paid at the Bank, omnibuses would still run, there would still be the old crush at the corner of Fenchurch Street.' All was of no avail. Nothing could moderate, in the bosom of the great English middle class, their passionate, absorbing, almost bloodthirsty, clinging to life.

MATTHEW ARNOLD.

And fear not lest Existence, closing your
Account and mine, shall know the like no more;
  The eternal Sáki from that Bowl has pour'd
Millions of Bubbles like us, and will pour.

FITZGERALD'S *Omar Khayyám.*

For honour travels in a strait so narrow,
Where one but goes abreast: keep then the path.

TROIL. AND CRESS. iii. 3.

I SAW then in my Dream, so far as this Valley reached, there was on the right hand a very deep Ditch; that Ditch is it into which the blind have led the blind in all Ages, and have both there miserably perished. Again, behold, on the left hand, there was a very dangerous Quag, into which, if even a good Man falls, he can find no bottom for his foot to stand on.

BUNYAN.

THAT thee is sent receive in buxomness,
The wrastling of this world asketh a fall;
Here is no home, here is but wilderness.
Forth, pilgrim, forth! forth, beast, out of thy stall!
Look up on high, and thankë God of all;
Waivë thy lust, and let thy ghost thee lead,
And Truth shall thee deliver, it is no dread.

CHAUCER.

—My Age is as a lusty winter,
Frosty, but kindly.

AS YOU LIKE IT ii. 3.

HIS life was playful from infancy to death, like the snow which in a calm day falls, but scarce seems to fall, and plays, and dances in and out till the very moment that it gently reaches the earth.

COLERIDGE.

THY thoughts and feelings shall not die,
Nor leave thee, when grey hairs are nigh,
A melancholy slave ;
But an old age serene and bright,
And lovely as a Lapland night,
Shall lead thee to thy grave.

WORDSWORTH.

Thou gaudy gold,
Hard food for Midas, I will none of thee.

MERCHANT OF VENICE iii. 2.

IT is a foolish thing that without money one cannot either live as one pleases, or where and with whom one pleases. Swift somewhere says that money is liberty; and I fear money is friendship too and society, and almost every external blessing. It is a great, though an ill-natured, comfort to see most of those who have it in plenty, without pleasure, without liberty, and without friends.

GRAY.

Art thou poor, yet hast thou golden slumbers?
O sweet content!
Art thou rich, yet is thy mind perplexèd?
O punishment!
Dost thou laugh to see how fools are vexèd
To add to golden numbers golden numbers?
O sweet content! O sweet, O sweet content!

DEKKER.

JANUARY 14

That thou art blam'd shall not be thy defect,
For slander's mark was ever yet the fair.

SONN. LXX.

INDEED I have always observed that women, whether out of a nicer regard to their honour, or what the reason I cannot tell, are more sensibly touched with those general expressions which are cast upon their sex, than men are by what is said of theirs.

STEELE.

—No fault in women, to refuse
The offer which they most would chuse.
—No fault in women, to confess
How tedious they are in their dress;
—No fault in women, to lay on
The tincture of vermilion,
And there to give the cheek a dye
Of white which Nature doth deny.
—No fault in women, though they be
But seldom from suspicion free;
—No fault in womenkind at all
If they but slip, and never fall!

HERRICK.

I had rather live
With cheese and garlic in a windmill, far,
Than feed on cates, and have him talk to me,
In any summer-house in Christendom.

I KING HENRY IV. iii. I.

BUT among such as deal in multitudes of words, none are comparable to the slow, deliberate talker, who proceedeth with much thought and caution, maketh his preface, brancheth out into several digressions, findeth a hint that putteth him in mind of another story, which he promiseth to tell you when this is done; cometh back regularly to his subject, cannot readily call to mind some person's name, holdeth his head, complaineth of his memory; the whole company all this while in suspense; at length, says he, it is no matter, and so goes on. And to crown the business, it perhaps proveth at last a story the company hath heard fifty times before; or, at best, some insipid adventure of the relater.

SWIFT.

WHAT man dare, I dare:
Approach thou like the rugged Russian bear,
The arm'd rhinoceros, or the Hyrcan tiger;
Take any shape but that, and my firm nerves
Shall never tremble.

MACBETH iii. 4.

To-morrow, and to-morrow, and to-morrow—

MACBETH V. 5.

THERE is no funeral so sad to follow as the funeral of our own youth, which we have been pampering with fond desires, ambitious hopes, and all the bright berries that hang in poisonous clusters over the path of life.

LANDOR.

O THAT I were an orange-tree,
That busy plant!
Then should I ever laden be,
And never want
Some fruit for Him that dresseth me.

But we are still too young or old;
The man is gone,
Before we do our wares unfold:
So we freeze on,
Until the grave increase our cold.

GEORGE HERBERT.

Will Fortune never come with both hands full?

2 KING HENRY IV. iv. 4.

IF I had no duties and no reference to futurity, I would spend my life in driving briskly in a post-chaise with a pretty woman; but she should be one who could understand me, and would add something to the conversation.

DR. JOHNSON.

CRABBED age and youth cannot live together:
Youth is full of pleasance, age is full of care;
Youth like summer morn, age like winter weather;
Youth like summer brave, age like winter bare.

The Passionate Pilgrim.

For I myself am best
When least in company.

TWELFTH NIGHT i. 4.

BUT the most ordinary cause of a Single Life, is Liberty; especially, in certain self-pleasing and humorous Minds, which are so sensible of every restraint, as they will go near, to think their Girdles, and Garters, to be Bonds and Shackles. Unmarried men are best Friends; best Masters; best Servants; but not always best Subjects: for they are light to run away; and almost all Fugitives are of that Condition.

BACON.

AH wretched, and too solitary he
Who loves not his own company:
He'll feel the weight of't many a day
Unless he call in sin or vanity
To help to bear 't away.

O Solitude, first state of humankind!
Which blest remain'd till man did find
Even his own helper's company.
As soon as two (alas!) together joined
The Serpent made up three.

COWLEY.

Remember
First to possess his books; for without them
He's but a sot, as I am.

TEMPEST iii. 2.

HERE were editions esteemed as being the first, and there stood others scarcely less regarded as being the last and best. Here was a book valued because it had the author's final improvements, and there another which (strange to tell!) was in request because it had them not. One was precious because it was a folio, another because it was a duodecimo; some because they were tall, some because they were short; the merit of this lay in the title-page, of that in the arrangement of the letters in the word Finis.

SCOTT.

THAT weight of wood, with leather coat o'erlaid,
Those awful clasps, of solid metal made,
The close-pressed leaves, unclosed for many an age,
The dull red edging of the well-filled page,
On the broad back the stubborn ridges rolled,
Where yet the title stands in tarnished gold;
These all a sage and laboured work proclaim,
A painful candidate for lasting fame;
No idle wit, no trifling verse can lurk
In the deep bosom of that weighty work.

CRABBE.

Be checked for silence,
But never taxed for speech.

ALL 'S WELL i. I.

LOOKING round on the noisy inanity of the world, words with little meaning, actions with little worth, one loves to reflect on the great empire of silence. The noble silent men, scattered here and there each in his department; silently thinking, silently working; whom no morning newspaper makes mention of!

CARLYLE.

BUT now, made free from them, next her before,
Peaceful and young, Herculean silence bore
His craggy club: which up aloft, he hild;
With which, and his fore-finger's charm, he still'd
All sounds in air, and left so free mine ears
That I might hear the music of the spheres,
And all the angels singing out of heaven.

CHAPMAN.

Small time, but in that small, most greatly liv'd
This star of England.

KING HENRY V. V. 2.

LET tyrants fear; I have always so behaved myself, that, under God, I have placed my chiefest strength and safeguard in the loyal hearts and goodwill of my subjects, and therefore I am come amongst you, as you see, at this time, not for my recreation and disport, but being resolved in the midst and heat of the battle to live or die amongst you all, to lay down for my God, and for my kingdoms, and for my people, my honour and my blood, even in the dust. I know I have the body but of a weak and feeble woman; but I have the heart and stomach of a king, and of a king of England too.

QUEEN ELIZABETH.

WHEN she did well, what did there else amiss?
When she did ill, what empires would have pleased?
No other power effecting woe or bliss,
She gave, she took, she wounded, she appeased.

RALEIGH.

Two loves I have, of comfort and despair.

SONN. CXLIV.

LOVE may be celestial fire before it enters into the system of mortals. It will then take the character of its place of abode, and we have to look not so much for the pure thing as for the passion.

GEORGE MEREDITH.

Love seeketh not itself to please,
  Nor for itself hath any care,
But for another gives its ease
  And builds a heaven in hell's despair.

Love seeketh only self to please,
  To bind another to its delight,
Joys in another's loss of ease,
  And builds a hell in heaven's despite.

BLAKE.

I have heard, but not believ'd, the spirits o' the dead
May walk again.

WINTER'S TALE iii. 3.

AND though it is most certain that two lutes being both strung and tuned to an equal pitch, and then one being played upon, the other that is not touched, being laid upon a table at a fit distance, will, like an echo to a trumpet, warble a faint audible harmony in answer to the same tune; yet many will not believe there is any such thing as a sympathy of souls; and I am well pleased that every reader do enjoy his own opinion.

IZAAK WALTON.

I LOOK for ghosts: but none will force
Their way to me; 'tis falsely said
That there was ever intercourse
Between the living and the dead:
For surely then I should have sight
Of him I wait for day and night
With love and longings infinite.

WORDSWORTH.

The players cannot keep counsel; they'll tell all.

HAMLET iii. 2.

NAY, the nature of this passion is so justly represented in a squinting little thief (who is always in a double action), that do but observe Clarissa next time you see her, and you will find, when her eyes have made their soft tour round the company, she makes no stay on him they say she is to marry, but rests two seconds of a minute on Wildair, who neither looks nor thinks on her or any woman else.

STEELE.

My lyre I tune, my voice I raise;
  But with my numbers mix my sighs:
And while I sing Euphelia's praise,
  I fix my soul on Chloe's eyes.

Fair Chloe blush'd: Euphelia frown'd:
  I sung, and gazed: I play'd, and trembled:
And Venus to the Loves around
  Remark'd, how ill we all dissembled.

PRIOR.

O gentlemen, the time of life is short;
To spend that shortness basely were too long.

I KING HENRY IV. V. 2.

IT has been well believed through many ages that the beginning of compunction is the beginning of a new life; that the mind which sees itself blameless may be called dead in trespasses—in trespasses on the love of others, in trespasses on their weakness, in trespasses on all those great claims which are the image of our own need.

GEORGE ELIOT.

GET up, get up, thou leaden man!
  Thy track, to endless joy or pain,
Yields but the model of a span:
  Yet burns out thy life's lamp in vain!
One minute bounds thy bane or bliss,
  Then watch and labour while time is!

CAMPION.

Had he his hurts before?
Ay, on the front.
Why, then, God's soldier be he!
MACBETH V. 8.

AND so farewell to the Christian hero, 'the happy warrior,' upon whom has come nothing which 'he did not foresee.' We, who are his countrymen, will cherish an affectionate remembrance of him while we live. We know that we cannot imitate the actions and characters of great men; we can only appreciate them: no effort of ours will place us on a level with them. Yet we pray also that some good influence may flow from them to us which may raise us above the conventionalities of the world, above the fashion of political opinions, to dwell in the light of justice, in the constancy of truth. And we pray for this nation also, that the lesson of a great man's death may not be lost upon us; but that in our public acts, as well as in our private lives, we may gather from him courage and firmness and wisdom and self-sacrifice and strength in all the trials which the English people may have to undergo in generations to come. JOWETT.

ONE man we knew, and only one,
Whose seeking for a city's done,
For what he greatly sought he found,
A city girt with fire around.

A city in an empty land
Between the wastes of sky and sand,
A city on a river-side
Where by the folk he loved he died.

A. LANG.

Why, all the souls that were, were forfeit once;
And he that might the vantage best have took
Found out the remedy.

MEASURE FOR MEASURE ii. 2.

THE old man told him that he worshipped the fire only, and acknowledged no other God; at which answer Abraham grew so jealously angry, that he thrust the old man out of his tent, and exposed him to all the evils of the night and an unguarded condition. When the old man was gone, God called to Abraham, and asked him where the stranger was. He replied, I thrust him away because he did not worship Thee: God answered him, I have suffered him these hundred years, although he dishonoured me; and couldst thou not endure him one night, when he gave thee no trouble?

JEREMY TAYLOR.

MUTUAL forgiveness of each vice,
Such are the gates of Paradise,
Against the Accuser's chief desire
Who walked among the stones of fire.

BLAKE.

Shall I not take mine ease in mine inn?

I KING HENRY IV. iii. 3.

THERE is no private house in which people can enjoy themselves so well as at a capital tavern. Let there be ever so great plenty of good things, ever so much grandeur, ever so much elegance, ever so much desire that everybody should be easy,—in the nature of things it cannot be: there must always be some degree of care and anxiety. The master of the house is anxious to entertain his guests; the guests are anxious to be agreeable to him; and no man, but a very impudent dog indeed, can as freely command what is in another man's house as if it were his own; whereas, at a tavern, there is a general freedom from anxiety. DR. JOHNSON.

HERE, waiter! take my sordid ore,
Which lacqueys else might hope to win;
It buys what Courts have not in store,
It buys me freedom, at an Inn.

Whoe'er has travell'd life's dull round,
Where'er his stages may have been,
May sigh to think how oft he found
The warmest welcome—at an Inn.

SHENSTONE.

O God, I could be bounded in a nutshell, and count myself a king of infinite space, were it not that I have bad dreams.

HAMLET ii. 2.

A MAN ought to be like a cunning actor, who, if he be enjoined to represent the person of some prince or nobleman, does it with a grace and comeliness; if, by and by, he be commanded to lay that aside and play the beggar, he does that as willingly and as well.

FULLER.

WERE I a king, I could command content;
Were I obscure, hidden should be my cares;
Or were I dead, no cares should me torment,
Nor hopes nor hates nor loves nor griefs nor
fears.
A doubtful choice, of these three which to crave,
A kingdom, or a cottage, or a grave.

E. VERE, EARL OF OXFORD.

You may my glories and my state depose,
But not my griefs; still am I king of those.

KING RICHARD II. iv. I.

HE walked across the park from the garden at St. James's that January morning with so firm and quick a pace that the guards could scarcely keep the step, and stepping from his own banqueting-house upon the scaffold, where the men who ruled England had so little understood him as to provide ropes and pulleys to drag him down in case of need, he died with that calm and kingly bearing which none could assume so well as he, and by his death he cast a halo of religious sentiment round a cause which, without the final act, would have wanted much of its pathetic charm, and struck the keynote of religious devotion to his person and the monarchy which has not yet ceased to reverberate in the hearts of men.

SHORTHOUSE.

HE nothing common did or mean,
Upon that memorable scene,
  But with his keener eye
  The axe's edge did try;
Nor called the gods with vulgar spite
To vindicate his helpless right,
  But bowed his comely head
  Down as upon a bed.

MARVELL.

JANUARY 31

I count myself in nothing else so happy
As in a soul remembering my good friends.

KING RICHARD II. ii. 3.

ALL that is left to us is to recommend our productions by the imitation of the Ancients; and it will be found true, that in every age, the highest character for sense and learning has been obtain'd by those who have been most indebted to them. For, to say truth, whatever is very good sense, must have been common sense in all times; and what we call Learning, is but the knowledge of the sense of our predecessors.

POPE.

How pleasing wears the wintry night,
Spent with the old illustrious dead!
While by the taper's trembling light
I seem those awful scenes to tread
Where chiefs or legislators lie
Whose triumphs move before my eye,
In arms and antique pomp arrayed;
While now I taste the Ionian song,
Now bend to Plato's god-like tongue
Resounding through the olive shade.

AKENSIDE.

FEBRUARY

Therefore, the poet
Did feign that Orpheus drew trees, stones, and floods.

MERCHANT OF VENICE V. I.

IS it nature, or by the error of fantasy, that the seeing of places we know to have been frequented or inhabited by men, whose memory is esteemed or mentioned in stories, doth in some sort move and stir us up as much or more than the hearing of their noble deeds, or reading of their compositions?

FLORIO'S *Montaigne.*

THEN old songs waken from enclouded tombs;
Old ditties sigh above their father's grave;
Ghosts of melodious prophesyings rave
Round every spot where trod Apollo's foot;
Bronze clarions awake, and faintly bruit,
Where long ago a giant battle was;
And from the turf a lullaby doth pass
In every place where infant Orpheus slept.

KEATS.

FEBRUARY 2

How far that little candle throws his beams!

MERCHANT OF VENICE V. I.

ANOTHER old custom there is, of saying, when light is brought in, *God sends us the light of Heaven*; and the parson likes this very well. Light is a great blessing, and as great as food, for which we give thanks: and those that think this superstitious, neither know superstition nor themselves.

GEORGE HERBERT.

MEN scarcely know how beautiful fire is—
  Each flame of it is as a precious stone
Dissolved in ever-moving light, and this
  Belongs to each and all who gaze upon.

SHELLEY.

What's yet in this,
That bears the name of life? Yet in this life
Lie hid moe thousand deaths.

MEASURE FOR MEASURE iii. I.

MEN that look no further than their outsides think health an appurtenance unto life, and quarrel with their constitutions for being sick; but I, that have examined the parts of man, and know upon what tender filaments that fabric hangs, do thank my God that we can die but once.

SIR THOMAS BROWNE.

DEVOURING Famine, Plague, and War,
Each able to undo mankind,
Death's servile emissaries are;
Nor to these alone confined,
He hath at will
More quaint and subtle ways to kill;
A smile or kiss, as he will use the art,
Shall have the cunning skill to break a heart.

SHIRLEY.

O undistinguished space of woman's will!

KING LEAR iv. 6.

CONSIDER with thyself, Fidus, that a fair woman without constancy is not unlike a green tree without fruit, resembling the counterfeit that Praxiteles made for Flora, before the which if one stood directly, it seemed to weep; if on the left side, to laugh; if on the other side, to sleep: whereby he noted the light behaviour of her, which could not in one constant shadow be set down.

LYLY.

It is not virtue, wisdom, valour, wit,
Strength, comeliness of shape, or amplest merit,
That woman's love can win or long inherit;
But what it is, hard is to say,
Harder to hit,
Which way soever men refer it,
Much like thy riddle, Samson, in one day
Or seven, though one should musing sit.

MILTON.

Nought so stockish, hard, and full of rage,
But music for the time doth change his nature.

MERCHANT OF VENICE V. I.

NOT all the tremulous voices of the flutes, not all the swift sighings of the violins, not all the noise of clanging trumpets or of shuddering drums, can equal or exhaust the splendour of our daily human joys, the throbbings of our loves, the quick pulsations of our fears, the nerveless sinking of our stricken hearts. The lovers that move on still evenings along the sheltering lanes, the mourners that creep back from a silent grave to a sullen and desolate home, these know more than all that storm of sound will ever say.

H. S. HOLLAND.

OH ! what is this that knows the road I came,
The flame turned cloud, the cloud returned to flame,
    The lifted shifted steeps and all the way ?—
That draws round me at last this wind-warm space,
And in regenerate rapture turns my face
    Upon the devious coverts of dismay ?

D. G. ROSSETTI.

Is she kind as she is fair,
For beauty lives with kindness?

TWO GENTLEMEN iv. 2.

NOT in vain—not in vain has he lived—hard and thankless should he be to think so—that has such a treasure given him. What is ambition compared to that, but selfish vanity? To be rich, to be famous? What do these profit a year hence, when other names sound louder than yours, when you lie hidden away under the ground, along with idle titles engraven on your coffin? But only true love lives after you—follows your memory with secret blessing—or precedes you, and intercedes for you.

THACKERAY.

Now sleep, and take thy rest,
  Once grieved and painèd wight,
Since she now loves thee best
  Who is thy heart's delight.
Let joy be thy soul's guest,
  And fear be banished quite,
Since she hath thee expressed
  To be her favourite.

JAMES MABBE.

It is not so with Him that all things knows,
As 'tis with us that square our guess by shows.

ALL'S WELL ii. I.

TO the common run of mankind it has always seemed a proof of mental vigour to find moral questions easy, and to judge conduct according to concise alternatives.

GEORGE ELIOT.

THINK not thy wisdom can illume away
The ancient tanglement of night and day.
Enough, to acknowledge both, and both revere:
They see not clearliest who see all things clear.

WILLIAM WATSON.

Under which king, Bezonian? Speak or die.

2 KING HENRY IV. V. 3.

WISE men are not violently attached to these things, nor do they violently hate them. Wisdom is not the most severe corrector of folly. They are the rival follies, which mutually wage so unrelenting a war; and which make so cruel a use of their advantages, as they can happen to engage the immoderate vulgar on the one side or the other in their quarrels.

BURKE.

My soul aches
To know, when two authorities are up,
Neither supreme, how soon confusion
May enter 'twixt the gap of both and take
The one by the other.

CORIOLANUS iii. I.

'Tis better to be lowly born,
And range with humble livers in content,
Than to be perk'd up in a glistering grief,
And wear a golden sorrow.

KING HENRY VIII. ii. 3.

FOR aught I see, they are as sick that surfeit with too much as they that starve with nothing. It is no mean happiness, therefore, to be seated in the mean: superfluity comes sooner by white hairs, but competency lives longer.

MERCHANT OF VENICE i. 2.

THERE is a jewel which no Indian mines
Can buy, no chymic art can counterfeit;
It makes men rich in greatest poverty,
Makes water wine, turns wooden cups to gold,
The homely whistle to sweet music's strain;
  Seldom it comes, to few from heaven sent,
  That much in little, all in naught, Content.

ANON.

Finding the first conceit of love there bred
Where time and outward form would show it dead.

SONN. CVIII.

IF it be true, that the Principal Part of Beauty, is in decent Motion, certainly it is no marvail, though Persons in Years, seem many times more Amiable: *Pulchrorum Autumnus pulcher*; For no Youth can be comely, but by Pardon, and considering the Youth, as to make up the Comeliness.

BACON.

No Spring nor Summer's Beauty hath such grace
As I have seen in one Autumnal Face.

DONNE.

For there is nothing either good or bad, but thinking makes it so.

HAMLET ii. 2.

I SAW a servant-maid, at the command of her mistress, make, kindle, and blow a fire. Which done, she was posted away about other business, whilst her mistress enjoyed the benefit of the fire. Yet I observed that this servant, whilst industriously employed in the kindling thereof, got a more general, kindly, and continuing heat than her mistress herself. Her heat was only by her, and not in her, staying with her no longer than she stayed by the chimney; whilst the warmth of the maid was inlaid, and equally diffused through the whole body.

FULLER.

As some rich woman, on a winter's morn,
Eyes through her silken curtains the poor drudge
Who with numb, blackened fingers makes her fire—
At cock-crow on a starlit winter's morn,
When the frost flowers the whitened window-panes—
And wonders how she lives, and what the thoughts
Of that poor drudge may be—

MATTHEW ARNOLD.

You jig, you amble, and you lisp, and nickname God's creatures, and make your wantonness your ignorance.

HAMLET iii. I.

I AM just come from visiting Sappho, a fine lady, who writes verses, sings, dances, and can say and do whatever she pleases, without the imputation of anything that can injure her character; for she is so well known to have no passion but self-love; or folly, but affectation; that now, upon any occasion, they only cry, 'It is her way!' and 'That is so like her!'

STEELE.

Wise Wretch! with Pleasures too refin'd to please;
With too much Spirit to be e'er at ease;
With too much Quickness ever to be taught;
With too much Thinking to have common Thought:
You purchase Pain with all that joy can give,
And die of nothing but a Rage to live.

POPE.

But what of this? are we not all in love?

LOVE'S LABOUR'S LOST iv. 3.

OPINION and Affection extremely differ. I may affect a Woman best, but it does not follow I must think her the handsomest Woman in the World. I love Apples best of any fruit, but it does not follow that I must think Apples to be the best fruit. Opinion is something wherein I go about to give reason why all the world should think as I think. Affection is a thing wherein I look after the pleasing of myself.

SELDEN.

It lies not in our power to love or hate,
For will in us is overruled by fate.
When two are stript, long ere the course begin,
We wish that one should lose, the other win;
And one especially I do affect
Of two gold ingots, like in each respect:
The reason no man knows; let it suffice,
What we behold is censured by our eyes.
Where both deliberate, the love is slight:
Who ever loved, that loved not at first sight?

MARLOWE.

And I a maid at your window,
To be your Valentine.

HAMLET iv. 5.

HAIL to thy returning festival, old Bishop Valentine! great is thy name in the rubric, thou venerable Arch-flamen of Hymen! Immortal go-between; who and what manner of person art thou? Art thou but a *name*, typifying the restless principle which impels poor humans to seek perfection in union? or wert thou indeed a mortal prelate, with thy tippet and thy rochet, thy apron on, and decent lawn sleeves?

CHARLES LAMB.

HAIL, Bishop Valentine, whose day this is;
All the air is thy diocese,
And all the chirping choristers
And other birds are thy parishioners:
Thou marriest every year
The lyric lark and the grave whispering dove,
The sparrow, that neglects his life for love,
The household bird with the red stomacher.

DONNE.

FEBRUARY 15

The little dogs and all,
Tray, Blanch, and Sweet-heart, see, they bark at me.
KING LEAR iii. 6.

BUT she, full of indignation and proud thoughts, made herself ready in all haste, and painted her face, hoping with her stately and imperious looks to daunt the Traitor, or at least to utter some Apophthegm that should express her brave spirit, and brand him with such a reproach as might make him odious for ever. Little did she think upon the hungry dogs that were ordained to devour her, whose paunches the *stibium,* with which she besmeared her eyes, would more offend, than the scolding language wherewith she armed her tongue could trouble the ears of him that had her in his power.

RALEIGH.

FAR less abhorred than these
Vexed Scylla bathing in the sea that parts
Calabria from the hoarse Trinacrian shore.

MILTON.

O mighty Cæsar, dost thou lie so low?
Are all thy conquests, glories, triumphs, spoils
Shrunk to this little measure?

JULIUS CÆSAR iii. I.

WHEN I look upon the tombs of the great, every emotion of envy dies in me; when I read the epitaphs of the beautiful, every inordinate desire goes out; when I meet with the grief of parents upon a tombstone, my heart melts with compassion; when I see the tomb of the parents themselves, I consider the vanity of grieving for those whom we must quickly follow. When I see kings lying by those who deposed them, when I consider rival wits placed side by side, or the holy men that divided the world with their contests and disputes, I reflect with sorrow and astonishment on the little competitions, factions, and debates of mankind. ADDISON.

HERE'S an acre sown indeed
With the richest, royallest seed
That the earth did e'er suck in
Since the first man died for sin:
Here the bones of birth have cried,
'Though gods they were, as men they died!'
Here are sands, ignoble things,
Dropped from the ruined sides of kings.

F. BEAUMONT.

As one, in suffering all, that suffers nothing;
A man, that fortune's buffets and rewards
Has ta'en with equal thanks.

HAMLET iii. 2.

'NOW, Mr. Tapley,' said Mark, giving himself a tremendous blow in the chest by way of reviver, 'just you attend to what I've got to say. Things is looking about as bad as they *can* look, young man. You'll not have such another opportunity for showing your jolly disposition, my fine fellow, as long as you live. And therefore, Tapley, Now's your time to come out strong; or Never!'

DICKENS.

GIVE me a man that is not dull,
When all the world with rifts is full;
But unamazed dares clearly sing,
Whenas the roof's a-tottering;
And, though it falls, continues still
Tickling the Cittern with his quill.

HERRICK.

A sullen bell
Remember'd knolling a departed friend.

2 KING HENRY IV. i. 1.

I BREAK in upon you at a moment when we least of all are permitted to disturb our friends, only to say, that you are daily and hourly present in my thoughts. If the worst be not yet past, you will neglect and pardon me; but if the last struggle be over; if the poor object of your long anxieties be no longer sensible to your kindness, or to her own sufferings, allow me (at least in idea, for what could I do, were I present, more than this?) to sit by you in silence, and pity from my heart, not her, who is at rest, but you, who lose her.

GRAY.

DWELL thou in endless light, discharged Soul,
Freed now from Nature's and from Fortune's trust;
While on this fluent Globe my Glass shall roll,
And run the rest of my remaining dust.

WOTTON.

Cowards die many times before their deaths;
The valiant never taste of death but once.

JULIUS CÆSAR ii. 2.

I HAVE so abject a conceit of this common way of existence, this retaining to the Sun and Elements, I cannot think this is to be a man, or to live according to the dignity of humanity; in expectation of a better, I can with patience embrace this life, yet in my best meditations do often defy death: I honour any man that contemns it, nor can I highly love any that is afraid of it: this makes me naturally love a Soldier, and honour those tattered and contemptible Regiments, that will die at the command of a Sergeant.

SIR THOMAS BROWNE.

Now farewell light, thou sunshine bright,
And all beneath the sky!
May coward shame distain his name,
The wretch that dares not die!

BURNS.

Ay, but to die, and go we know not where.

MEASURE FOR MEASURE iii. 1.

I AM not content to pass away like a weaver's shuttle. These metaphors solace me not, nor sweeten the unpalatable draught of mortality. I care not to be carried with the tide, and reluct at the inevitable course of destiny. I am in love with this green earth; the face of town and country; the unspeakable rural solitudes, and the sweet security of streets.

CHARLES LAMB.

For who, to dumb forgetfulness a prey,
  This pleasing, anxious being e'er resign'd,
Left the warm precincts of the cheerful day,
  Nor cast one longing, lingering look behind?

GRAY.

Unless things mortal move them not at all.

HAMLET ii. 2.

BUT the dead *genii* were satisfied with little—a few violets—a cake dipped in wine, or a morsel of honeycomb. Daily, from the time when his childish footsteps were still uncertain, had Marius taken them their portion of the family meal, at the second course, amidst the silence of the company. They loved those who brought them their sustenance; but, deprived of those services, would be heard wandering through the house, crying sorrowfully in the stillness of the night.

WALTER PATER.

IN consecrated earth,
And on the holy hearth,
The Lars and Lemures moan with mid-
night plaint;
In urns, and altars round,
A drear and dying sound—

MILTON.

And beauty making beautiful old rhyme,
In praise of ladies dead and lovely knights.

SONN. CVI.

THERE are chapels in the cathedral of man's highest art as in that of his inmost life, not made to be set open to the eyes and feet of the world. Love and death and memory keep charge for us in silence of some beloved names. It is the crowning glory of genius, the final miracle and transcendent gift of poetry, that it can add to the number of these, and engrave on the very heart of our remembrance fresh names and memories of its own creation.

SWINBURNE.

BLESSINGS be with them, and eternal praise,
Who gave us nobler loves, and nobler cares—
The poets, who on earth have made us heirs
Of truth and pure delight by heavenly lays!
O might my name be numbered among theirs,
Then gladly would I end my mortal days.

WORDSWORTH.

Glory is like a circle in the water,
Which never ceaseth to enlarge itself,
Till, by broad spreading, it disperse to nought.

I KING HENRY VI. i. 2.

THESE fingers of lamplight, struggling up through smoke and thousandfold exhalation, some fathoms into the ancient reign of night, what thinks Boötes of them, as he leads his Hunting-dogs over the Zenith in their leash of sidereal fire?

CARLYLE.

Thus those celestial fires,
Though seeming mute,
The fallacy of our desires,
And all the pride of life, confute.

For they have watched since first
The world had birth,
And found sin in itself accurst,
And nothing permanent on earth.

HABINGTON.

It were all one
That I should love a bright particular star,
And think to wed it.

ALL'S WELL i. 1.

AND from hence it is that for the most part they have much better fortune in love whose hopes are built on something in their person than those that trust to their expressions and service; and they that care less than they that care more: which not perceiving, many men cast away their services as one arrow after another, till, in the end, together with their hopes, they lose their wits.

HOBBES.

Sleep, sleep again, my lyre!
For thou canst never tell my humble tale
In sounds that may prevail,
Nor gentle thoughts in her inspire;
All thy vain mirth lay by,
Bid thy strings silent lie,
Sleep, sleep again, my lyre, and let thy master
die.

COWLEY.

And make a moral of the devil himself.

KING HENRY V. iv. I.

I DECLARE, quoth my uncle Toby, my heart would not let me curse the D——l himself with so much bitterness. . . . He is the father of curses, replied Dr. Slop. . . . So am not I, replied my uncle. But he is cursed and damned already to all eternity, replied Dr. Slop. I am sorry for it, quoth my uncle Toby.

STERNE.

But, fare you weel, auld Nickie-ben!
O wad ye tak' a thought an' men'!
Ye aiblins might—I dinna ken—
Still hae a stake—
I 'm wae to think upo' yon den,
Ev'n for your sake!

BURNS.

Falseness cannot come from thee, for thou lookst
Modest as Justice, and thou seemst a palace
For the crown'd Truth to dwell in.

PERICLES V. I.

IN this accomplished lady love is the constant effect, because it is never the design. Yet, though her mien carries much more invitation than command, to behold her is an immediate check to loose behaviour; and to love her is a liberal education.

STEELE.

Ye meaner beauties of the night,
  That poorly satisfy our eyes
More by your number than your light,
  You common people of the skies,
What are you, when the Moon shall rise?

WOTTON.

O sleep, O gentle sleep,
Nature's soft nurse—

2 KING HENRY IV. iii. I.

YEA, so greatly indebted are we to this kinsman of death, that we owe the better tributary, half of our life to him: and there is good cause why we should do so: for sleep is that golden chain that ties health and our bodies together. Who complains of want? of wounds? of cares? of great men's oppressions? of captivity? whilst he sleepeth? Beggars in their beds take as much pleasure as kings: can we therefore surfeit on this delicate ambrosia? Can we drink too much of that whereof to taste too little tumbles us into a churchyard, and to use it indifferently throws us into Bedlam? No, no, look on Endymion, the moon's minion, who slept threescore and fifteen years, and was not a hair the worse for it. Can lying abed till noon (being not the threescore and fifteenth thousand part of his nap) be hurtful?

DEKKER.

TAKE thou of me sweet pillows, sweetest bed,
A chamber deaf to noise, and blind to light,
A rosy garland, and a weary head.

PHILIP SIDNEY.

FEBRUARY 28

Be to yourself
As you would to your friend.

KING HENRY VIII. i. 1.

'THE theatre of all my actions is fallen,' said an antique personage when his chief friend was dead; and they are fortunate who get a theatre where the audience demands their best.

GEORGE ELIOT.

AND if thou cast thine eyes below,
  How dimly character'd and slight,
  How dwarf'd a growth of cold and night,
How blanch'd with darkness must I grow!

Yet turn thee to the doubtful shore,
  Where first thy form was made a man,
  I loved thee, Spirit, and love, nor can
The soul of Shakspeare love thee more.

TENNYSON.

I wish'd myself a man,
Or that we women had men's privilege
Of speaking first.

TROIL. AND CRESS. iii. 2.

'AFRAID! why should I be afraid? John! My own John! Mamma, he is my own.' And she put out her arms to him, as though calling him to come to her. Things were now very bad with John Eames,—so bad that he would have given a considerable lump out of Lord de Guest's legacy to be able to escape at once into the street. The power of a woman, when she chooses to use it recklessly, is for the moment almost unbounded.

ANTHONY TROLLOPE.

RUN when you will, the story shall be changed;
Apollo flies, and Daphne holds the chase;
The dove pursues the griffin; the mild hind
Makes speed to catch the tiger; bootless speed,
When cowardice pursues and valour flies.

MIDSUMMER-NIGHT'S DREAM ii. 1.

MARCH

MARCH I

Time hath, my lord, a wallet at his back,
Wherein he puts alms for oblivion.

TROIL. AND CRESS. iii. 3.

SOLOMON saith: there is no New Thing upon the Earth. So that as Plato had an Imagination; that all Knowledge was but Remembrance; so Solomon giveth his Sentence; That all Novelty is but Oblivion. Whereby you may see, that the River of Lethe runneth as well above Ground, as below.

BACON.

TRUTH fails not; but her outward forms that bear
The longest date do melt like frosty rime,
That in the morning whitened hill and plain
And is no more; drop like the tower sublime
Of yesterday, which royally did wear
His crown of weeds, but could not even sustain
Some casual shout that broke the silent air,
Or the unimaginable touch of Time.

WORDSWORTH.

Who were below him
He used as creatures of another place;
And bow'd his eminent top to their low ranks,
Making them proud of his humility.

ALL'S WELL i. 2.

IT is almost a definition of a gentleman to say that he is one who never inflicts pain. . . . He has his eyes on all his company; he is tender towards the bashful, gentle towards the distant, and merciful towards the absurd. He can recollect to whom he is speaking; he guards against unseasonable allusions, or topics which may irritate; he is seldom prominent in conversation, and never wearisome. . . . He is never mean or little in his disputes, never takes unfair advantage, never mistakes personalities or sharp sayings for arguments, or insinuates evil which he dare not say out.

CARDINAL NEWMAN.

Look who that is most virtuous alway,
Prive and apert, and most entendeth aye
To do the gentle dedës that he can,
And take him for the greatest gentleman.

CHAUCER.

Death lies on her, like an untimely frost
Upon the sweetest flower of all the field.

ROMEO AND JULIET iv. 4.

THE beauteous virgin! how ignorantly did she charm, how carelessly excel! O Death! thou hast right to the bold, to the ambitious, to the high, and to the haughty; but why this cruelty to the humble, to the meek, to the undiscerning, to the thoughtless? Nor age, nor business, nor distress, can erase the dear image from my imagination. In the same week, I saw her dressed for a ball, and in a shroud. How ill did the habit of death become the pretty trifler! I still behold the smiling earth—

STEELE.

LOVE, what ailed thee to leave life that was made
lovely, we thought, with love?
What sweet visions of sleep lured thee away, down
from the light above?

What strange faces of dreams, voices that called,
hands that were raised to wave,
Lured or led thee, alas! out of the sun, down to
the sunless grave?

SWINBURNE.

I am no great Nebuchadnezzar, sir; I have not much skill in grass. ALL'S WELL iv. 5.

AFTER several parallels between great men, which appeared to me altogether groundless and chimerical, I was surprised to hear one say, that he valued the Black Prince more than the Duke of Vendosme. How the Duke of Vendosme should become a rival of the Black Prince, I could not conceive: and was more startled when I heard a second affirm with great vehemence, that if the Emperor of Germany was not going off, he should like him better than either of them. He added that though the season was so changeable, the Duke of Marlborough was in blooming beauty.

ADDISON.

—NATURE is made better by no mean,
But nature makes that mean: so, over that art,
Which, you say, adds to nature, is an art
That nature makes. You see, sweet maid, we marry
A gentler scion to the wildest stock;
And make conceive a bark of baser kind
By bud of nobler race: This is an art
Which does mend nature,—change it rather: but
The art itself is nature.

WINTER'S TALE iv. 4.

To live a barren sister all your life,
Chanting faint hymns to the cold fruitless moon.

MIDSUMMER-NIGHT'S DREAM i. 1.

NO lording husband shall at the same time command her presence and distance; to be always near in constant attendance, and always stand aloof in awful observance.

FULLER.

HE was a poet, sure a lover too,
Who stood on Latmos' top, what time there blew
Soft breezes from the myrtle vale below,
And brought in faintness solemn, sweet, and slow,
A hymn from Dian's temple; while upswelling,
The incense went to her own starry dwelling.
But though her face was clear as infant's eyes,
Though she stood smiling o'er the sacrifice,
The poet wept at her so piteous fate,
Wept that such beauty should be desolate,
So in fine wrath some golden sounds he won,
And gave meek Cynthia her Endymion.

KEATS.

But that I love the gentle Desdemona
I would not my unhousèd free condition
Put into circumscription and confine
For the sea's worth.

OTHELLO i. 2.

'TIS just like a summer bird-cage in a garden: the birds that are without despair, to get in, and the birds that are within despair, and are in a consumption, for fear they shall never get out.

WEBSTER.

So bitter is their sweet that True Content
Unhappy men in them can never find:
Ah! but without them, none. Both must consent,
Else uncouth are the joys of either kind.
Let us then praise their good, forget their ill!
Men must be men, and women women still.

CAMPION.

MARCH 7

For stony limits cannot hold love out.

ROMEO AND JULIET ii. 2.

DURING the time of his imprisonment, I failed not constantly to go, when the clock struck four in the morning, with a dark lantern in my hand, all alone and on foot, from my lodging in Chancery Lane, at my cousin Young's, to Whitehall, in at the entry that went out of King Street, into the bowling-green. There I would go under his window and softly call him: he, after the first time excepted, never failed to put out his head at the first call: thus we talked together, and sometimes I was so wet with the rain, that it went in at my neck and out at my heels.

LADY FANSHAWE.

WHEN Love with unconfinèd wings
  Hovers within my gates,
And my divine Althea brings
  To whisper at the grates;
When I lie tangled in her hair,
  And fetter'd to her eye,
The Gods that wanton in the air
  Know no such liberty.

LOVELACE.

Your wit 's too hot, it speeds too fast, 'twill tire.
LOVE'S LABOUR 'S LOST ii. I.

NOT only the fame of Marcellus, but every other, *crescit occulto velut arbor aevo*; and that which makes the greatest vernal shoot is apt to make the least autumnal. Authors in general who have met celebrity at starting, have already had their reward; always their utmost due, and often much beyond it. We cannot hope for both celebrity and fame: supremely fortunate are the few who are allowed the liberty of choice between them.

LANDOR.

If hence thy silence be
As 'tis too just a cause;
Let this thought quicken thee:
Minds that are great and free
Should not on fortune pause,
'Tis crown enough to virtue still, her own applause.

BEN JONSON.

O, and is all forgot?
All school-days' friendship, childhood innocence?
MIDSUMMER-NIGHT'S DREAM iii. 2.

IN the morning of our days, when the senses are unworn and tender, when the whole man is awake in every part, and the gloss of novelty fresh upon all the objects that surround us, how lively at that time are our sensations, but how false and inaccurate the judgments we form of things! I despair of ever receiving the same degree of pleasure from the most excellent performances of genius, which I felt at that age from pieces which my present judgment regards as trifling and contemptible. BURKE.

AN idle poet, here and there,
Looks round him: but, for all the rest
The world, unfathomably fair,
Is duller than a witling's jest.
Love wakes men, once a lifetime each;
They lift their heavy eyes, and look;
And, lo, what one sweet page can teach,
They read with joy, then shut the book.
And some give thanks, and some blaspheme,
And most forget; but, either way,
That and the Child's unheeded dream
Is all the light of all their day.

COVENTRY PATMORE.

MARCH 10

Daffodils,
That come before the swallow dares, and take
The winds of March with beauty.

WINTER'S TALE iv. 3.

AS to myself, I cannot boast, at present, either of my spirits, my situation, my employments, or fertility. The days and the nights pass, and I am never the nearer to anything, but that one to which we are all tending; yet I love people that leave some traces of their journey behind them, and have strength enough to advise you to do so while you can.

GRAY.

FAIR daffodils, we weep to see
You haste away so soon;
As yet the early-rising sun
Has not attained his noon.
Stay, stay,
Until the hasting day
Has run
But to the evensong;
And, having pray'd together, we
Will go with you along.

HERRICK.

MARCH 11

When in the chronicle of wasted time
I see descriptions of the fairest wights—

SONN. CVI.

AH, Launcelot, he said, thou wert head of all Christian knights: and now, I dare say, said Sir Ector, thou Sir Launcelot, there thou liest, that thou were never matched of earthly knight's hand; and thou were the courtliest knight that ever bare shield; and thou were the truest friend to thy lover that ever bestrode horse; and thou were the truest lover of a sinful man that ever loved woman; and thou were the kindest man that ever strake with sword; and thou were the goodliest person that ever came among press of knights; and thou was the meekest man and the gentlest that ever ate in hall among ladies; and thou were the sternest knight to thy mortal foe that ever put spear in the rest.

MALORY.

RIGHT valiant was he,
God's body to see,
Though he saw it not.
Right valiant to move,
But for his sad love,
The high God above
Stinted his praise.

WILLIAM MORRIS.

See that you come
Not to woo honour, but to wed it.

ALL'S WELL ii. I.

LOOKING on the chapel of King Henry VII. in Westminster (God grant I may once again see it, with the Saint who belongs to it, our sovereign, there in a well-conditioned peace), I say, looking on the outside of the chapel, I have much admired the curious workmanship thereof. It added to the wonder, that it is so shadowed with mean houses, well-nigh on all sides, that one may almost touch it as soon as see it. Such a structure needed no base buildings about it, as foils to set it off. Rather this chapel may pass for the emblem of a great worth; living in a private way. How is he pleased with his own obscurity, while others of less desert make greater show!

FULLER.

VAIN honour! thou art but disguise,
A cheating voice, a juggling art;
No judge of virtue, whose pure eyes
Court her own image in the heart,
More pleased with her true figure there
Than her false echo in the ear.

CAREW.

For in that sleep of death what dreams may come—
HAMLET iii. I.

AND of all that range of sentiment he (Michel Angelo) is the poet, a poet still alive and in possession of our inmost thoughts—dumb inquiry, the relapse after death into the formlessness which preceded life, change, revolt from that change, then the correcting, hallowing, consoling rush of pity; at last, far off, thin and vague, yet not more vague than the most definite thoughts men have had through three centuries on a matter that has been so near their hearts—the new body: a passing light, a mere intangible, external effect over those too rigid or too formless faces; a dream that lingers a moment, retreating in the dawn, incomplete, aimless, helpless; a thing with faint hearing, faint memory, faint power of touch; a breath, a flame in the doorway, a feather in the wind.

WALTER PATER.

I DARE not guess; but in this life
Of error, ignorance, and strife,
Where nothing is, but all things seem,
And we the shadows of a dream:
It is a modest creed, and yet
Pleasant, if one considers it,
To own that death itself must be
Like all the rest, a mockery.

SHELLEY.

The beggar's nurse and Cæsar's.

ANT. AND CLEOP. V. 2.

O ELOQUENT, just, and mighty Death! whom none could advise, thou hast persuaded: what none hath dared, thou hast done; and whom the world hath flattered, thou only hast cast out of the world and despised: thou hast drawn together all the far-stretched greatness, all the pride, cruelty, and ambition of man, and covered it over with these two narrow words: *Hic Jacet.*

RALEIGH.

THEY say the Lion and the Lizard keep
The courts where Jamshyd gloried and drank deep:
And Bahrám, that great Hunter—the Wild Ass
Stamps o'er his Head, but cannot break his Sleep.

FITZGERALD'S *Omar Khayyám.*

Who is it that says most? which can say more
Than this rich praise,—that you alone are you?

SONN. LXXXIV.

CERTAINLY, Fame is like a River, that beareth up Things light and swoln, and drowns Things weighty and solid. But if persons of quality and judgment concur, then it is (as the Scripture saith), *Nomen bonum instar unguenti fragrantis.* It filleth all round about, and will not easily away. For the Odours of Ointments are more Durable than those of Flowers.

BACON.

DOUBT you to whom my Muse these notes intendeth;
Which now my breast o'ercharged to music lendeth?
  To you! to you! all song of praise is due:
Only in you my soul begins and endeth.

Who hath the eyes which marry state with pleasure,
Who keeps the keys of nature's chiefest treasure?
  To you! to you! all song of praise is due:
Only for you the heaven forgat all measure.

PHILIP SIDNEY.

There lives within the very flame of love
A kind of wick, or snuff, that will abate it.

HAMLET iv. 7.

TOO late their eyes are opened: they were taken unawares and desire to part company. Better, he would say, a 'little love at the beginning,' for heaven might have increased it; but now their foolish fondness has changed into mutual dislike. In the days of their honeymoon they never understood that they must provide against offences, that they must have interests, that they must learn the art of living as well as loving. Our misogamist will not appeal to Anacreon or Sappho for a confirmation of his view, but to the universal experience of mankind.

JOWETT.

When passion's trance is overpast,
If tenderness and truth could last
Or live, whilst all wild feelings keep
Some mortal slumber, dark and deep,
I should not weep, I should not weep!

SHELLEY.

The poet's eye in a fine frenzy rolling
Doth glance from heaven to earth, from earth to heaven.

MIDSUMMER-NIGHT'S DREAM V. I.

I AM convinced more and more, every day, that fine writing is, next to fine doing, the top thing in the world; the 'Paradise Lost' becomes a greater wonder. The more I know what my diligence may in time probably effect, the more does my heart distend with pride and obstinacy. . . . My own being, which I know to be, becomes of more consequence to me than the crowds of shadows in the shape of men and women that inhabit a kingdom. The soul is a world of itself, and has enough to do in its own home. KEATS.

If all the pens that ever poets held
Had fed the feeling of their master's thoughts,
And every sweetness that inspired their hearts,
Their minds, and muses, on admirèd themes;
If all the heavenly quintessence they 'still
From the immortal flowers of poesy,
Wherein as in a mirror we perceive
The highest reaches of a human wit;
If these had made one poem's period,
And all combined in beauty's worthiness,
Yet should there hover in their restless heads
One thought, one grace, one wonder at the least
Which into words no virtue can digest.

MARLOWE.

Call me what instrument you will, though you can fret me, yet you cannot play upon me.

HAMLET iii. 2.

A DISTINCT universe walks about under your hat and under mine—all things in nature are different to each—the woman we look at has not the same features, the dish we eat from has not the same taste to the one and the other—you and I are but a pair of infinite isolations, with some fellow-islands a little more or less near to us.

THACKERAY.

Who order'd that their longing's fire
Should be, as soon as kindled, cool'd?
Who renders vain their deep desire?—
A God, a God their severance ruled!
And bade between their shores to be
The unplumb'd, salt, estranging sea.

MATTHEW ARNOLD.

Doth not rosemary and Romeo begin both with a letter?

ROMEO AND JULIET ii. 4.

AND it could not taste of death, by reason of its adoption into immortal palaces; but it was to know weakness, and reliance, and the shadow of human imbecility; and it went with a lame gait; but in its goings it exceeded all mortal children in grace and swiftness. Then pity first sprang up in angelic bosoms; and yearnings (like the human) touched them at the sight of the immortal lame one.

CHARLES LAMB.

HUSH! my heedless feet from under
  Slip the crumbling banks for ever:
Like echoes to a distant thunder,
  They plunge into the gentle river.
The river-swans have heard my tread,
  And startle from their reedy bed.
O beauteous birds, methinks ye measure
  Your movements to some heavenly tune!
O beauteous birds! 'tis such a pleasure
  To see you move beneath the moon,
I would it were your true delight
  To sleep by day and wake all night.

COLERIDGE.

ARCH 20

Ditties highly penn'd
Sung by a fair queen in a summer's bower,
With ravishing division, to her lute.

I KING HENRY IV. iii. I.

I BELIEVE I can tell the particular little chance that filled my head first with such chimes of verse, as have never since left ringing there; for I remember, when I began to read, and take some pleasure in it, there was wont to lie in my mother's parlour (I know not by what accident, for she herself never in her life read any book but of devotion;) but there was wont to lie Spenser's Works; this I happened to fall upon, and was infinitely delighted with the stories of the knights and giants, and monsters, and brave horses which I found everywhere there (though my understanding had little to do with all this); and by degrees, with the tinkling of the rhyme, and dance of the numbers, so that I had read him all before I was twelve years old, and was thus made a poet.

COWLEY.

To his sweet lute Apollo sang the motions of the spheres,
The wondrous order of the stars whose course divides the years,
And all the mysteries above;
But none of this could Midas move:
Which purchased him his ass's ears.

CAMPION.

If I had my liberty, I would do my liking.

MUCH ADO i. 3.

THERE is written on the Turrets of the City of *Luca* in great characters at this day, the word LIBERTAS: Yet no man can thence infer, that a particular man has more Liberty, or Immunity from the service of the Commonwealth there, than in Constantinople.

HOBBES.

SEEING this vale, this earth, on which we dream
Is on all sides o'ershadowed by the high
Uno'erleap'd mountains of Necessity,
Sparing us narrower margin than we deem.

MATTHEW ARNOLD.

Thou know'st, the first time that we smell the air,
We wawl, and cry.

KING LEAR iv. 6.

THE Thracians wept when a child was born, and feasted and made merry when a man went out of the world, and with reason. Is it not better not to hunger at all, than to eat? Not to thirst, than to take physic to cure it? Is it not better to be freed from cares and agues, love and melancholy, and all the other hot and cold fits of life, than, like a galled traveller, who comes weary to his inn, to be bound to begin his journey afresh?

STERNE.

IN this world, the Isle of Dreams,
While we sit by sorrow's streams,
Tears and terrors are our themes
Reciting.

HERRICK.

MARCH 23

Put out the light, and then—put out the light.

OTHELLO V. 2.

SOLEMN indeed is the place, solemn and strangely suggestive, for the simple reason that we shall scarcely find four walls elsewhere that enclose within a like area an equal quantity of genius. The air is thick with it, and dense and difficult to breathe; for it was genius that was not happy, inasmuch as it lacked the art to fix itself for ever. It is not immortality that we breathe at the Scuola di San Rocco, but conscious, reluctant mortality.

HENRY JAMES.

—WHAT would one have?
In heaven, perhaps, more chances, one more
chance,—
Four great walls in the new Jerusalem
Meted on each side by the angel's reed,
For Leonard, Rafael, Agnolo and me
To cover—

BROWNING.

Prosper this realm, keep it from civil broils.

I KING HENRY VI. i. I.

HE that goeth about to persuade a multitude that they are not so well governed as they ought to be, shall never want attentive and favourable hearers; because they know the manifold defects, whereunto every kind of regiment is subject, but the secret lets and difficulties, which in public proceedings are innumerable and inevitable, they have not ordinarily the judgment to consider. And because such as openly reprove supposed disorders of state are taken for principal friends to the common benefit of all, and for men that carry singular freedom of mind, under this fair and plausible colour whatsoever they utter, passeth for good and current.

HOOKER.

WELL, if a King 's a Lion, at the least
The People are a many-headed beast:
Can they direct what measures to pursue,
Who know themselves so little what to do?

POPE.

Now, God be praised, that to believing souls
Gives light in darkness, comfort in despair.

2 KING HENRY VI. ii. 1.

WE entered upon the moor, and had advanced about a mile when dark night fell around us; we were in a wild path, with high brushwood on either side, when the rider said that he could not confront the darkness, and begged me to ride on before, and he would follow after: I could hear him trembling. I asked the reason of his terror, and he replied that at one time darkness was the same thing to him as day, but that of late years he dreaded it, especially in wild places. I complied with his request, but I was ignorant of the way, and as I could scarcely see my hand, was continually going wrong. This made the man impatient, and he again placed himself at our head. We proceeded so a considerable way, when he again stopped, and said that the power of the darkness was too much for him. His horse seemed to be infected with the same panic, for it shook in every limb.

GEORGE BORROW.

THE wheel of Fortune guide you,
The boy with the bow beside you
Run aye in the way
Till the bird of day
And the luckier lot betide you!

BEN JONSON.

MARCH 26

Hence from Verona art thou banished:
Be patient, for the world is broad and wide.

ROMEO AND JULIET iii. 3.

ANOTHER misery there is in affection; that whom we truly love like our own selves, we forget their looks, nor can our memory retain the idea of their faces; and it is no wonder, for they are ourselves, and our affection makes their looks our own.

SIR THOMAS BROWNE.

By absence this good means I gain,
 That I can catch her,
 Where none can watch her,
In some close quarter of my brain:
 There I embrace and kiss her;
And so I both enjoy and miss her.

DONNE.

His horses are bred better; for, besides that they are fair with their feeding, they are taught their manage.

AS YOU LIKE IT i. 1.

IT is a pity that commonly more care is had, and that among very wise men, to find out a cunning man for their horse, than a cunning man for their children. To the one they will gladly give a stipend of 200 crowns by the year, and loth to offer the other 200 shillings. God, that sitteth in heaven, laugheth their choice to scorn, and rewardeth their liberality as it should; for He suffereth them to have tame and well-ordered horse, but wild and unfortunate children.

ASCHAM.

THIS loss springs chiefly from our education.
Some till their ground, but let weeds choke their
son:
Some mark a partridge, never their child's fashion:
Some ship them over; and the thing is done.
Study this art; make it thy great design;
And if God's image move thee not, let thine.

GEORGE HERBERT.

Give me that man that is not passion's slave.

HAMLET iii. 2.

THESE, sensual men thought mad, because they would not be partakers or practisers of their madness. But they, placed high on the top of all virtue, looked down on the stage of the world, and contemned the play of fortune. For, though the most be players, some must be spectators.

BEN JONSON.

AND whilst distraught ambition compasses,
And is encompass'd; whilst as craft deceives,
And is deceived: whilst man doth ransack man
And builds on blood, and rises by distress;
And th' inheritance of desolation leaves
To great-expecting hopes: he looks thereon
As from the shore of peace, with unwet eye,
And bears no venture in impiety.

DANIEL.

All places that the eye of heaven visits
Are to a wise man ports and happy havens.

KING RICHARD II. i. 3.

I PITY the man that can travel from *Dan* to *Beersheba*, and cry, 'tis all barren—and so it is; and so is all the world to him who will not cultivate the fruits it offers.

STERNE.

NATURE, so far as in her lies,
Imitates God, and turns her face
To every land beneath the skies,
Counts nothing that she meets with base,
But lives and loves in every place.

TENNYSON.

Here's a few flowers; but 'bout midnight, more:
The herbs that have on them cold dew o' the night.

CYMBELINE iv. 2.

LOVED ones are taken away, and the boy, the girl, will not speak of them, as if that made the conqueror's triumph the less. In time the fire in the breast burns low, and then in the last glow of the embers, it is sweeter to hold to what has been than to think of what may be.

J. M. BARRIE.

THERE scattered oft, the earliest of the year,
By hands unseen are showers of violets found;
The redbreast loves to build and warble there,
And little footsteps lightly print the ground.

GRAY.

To this I am most constant
Though destiny say no.

WINTER'S TALE iv. 4.

AND the past, and its dear histories, and youth and its hopes and passions, and tones and looks, for ever echoing in the heart and present in the memory—these, no doubt, poor Clive saw and heard as he looked across the great gulf of time and parting and grief, and beheld the woman he had loved for many years.

THACKERAY.

THOUGH seas and land betwixt us both,
Our faith and troth
(Like separated souls)
All time and space controls:
Above the highest sphere we meet
Unseen, unknown, and greet as Angels greet.

LOVELACE.

APRIL

Call me not fool till heaven hath sent me fortune.

AS YOU LIKE IT ii. 7.

MEN of genius are rarely much annoyed by the company of vulgar people, because they have a power of looking *at* such persons as objects of amusement of another race altogether.

COLERIDGE.

Fools, they are the only nation
Worth men's envy or admiration;
Free from care or sorrow-taking,
Selves and others merry-making:
All they speak or do is sterling,
Your fool he is your great man's darling,
And your lady's sport and pleasure;
Tongue and bauble are his Treasure;
Even his face begetteth laughter—

BEN JONSON.

The uncertain glory of an April day.

TWO GENTLEMEN i. 3.

ELEGANTLY doth this Flower [narcissus], appearing in the beginning of the Spring, represent the likeness of these Men's dispositions, who, in their Youth do flourish and wax famous; but being come to ripeness of Years, they deceive and frustrate the good Hope that is conceived of them. Neither is it impertinent that this Flower is said to be consecrated to the infernal Deities, because Men of this disposition become unprofitable to all Human Things: For whatsoever produceth no Fruit of itself, but passeth, and vanisheth as if it had never been (like the way of a Ship in the Sea), that the ancients were wont to dedicate to the Ghosts and Powers below.

BACON.

WEEP no more, nor sigh, nor groan,
Sorrow calls no time that 's gone;
Violets plucked the sweetest rain
Makes not fresh nor grow again.

FLETCHER.

APRIL 3

The April's in her eyes: it is love's spring.

ANT. AND CLEOP. iii. 2.

THESE abstractions from his studies, excesses of gaiety, and glumness, heavings of the chest, and other odd signs, but mainly the disgusting behaviour of his pupil at the dinner-table, taught Adrian to understand, though the young gentleman was clever in excuses, that he had somehow learnt there was another half to the divided Apple of Creation, and had embarked upon the great voyage of discovery of the difference between the two halves.

GEORGE MEREDITH.

AH, I remember well (and how can I
But evermore remember well) when first
Our flame began, when scarce we knew what was
The flame we felt; when as we sat and sighed
And looked upon each other, and conceived
Not what we ail'd—yet something we did ail;
And yet were well, and yet we were not well,
And what was our disease we could not tell.

DANIEL.

Love comforteth like sunshine after rain.

VENUS AND ADONIS.

I AM particularly pleased with a passage in Homer, wherein Jupiter is represented as taking off his eyes, with a sort of satiety, from the horror of the field of battle, and relieving himself with a view of the Hippomolgi, a people famous, it seems, for their innocence and simplicity of manners.

MELMOTH.

Wise men patience never want,
Good men pity cannot hide;
Feeble spirits only vaunt
Of revenge, the poorest pride:
He alone forgive that can
Bears the true soul of a man.

Deeds from love and words that flow
Foster like kind April showers;
In the warm sun all things grow,
Wholesome fruits and pleasant flowers:
All so thrives his gentle rays
Whereon human love displays.

CAMPION.

APRIL 5

If consequence do but approve my dream.

OTHELLO ii. 3.

OFTEN I used to see, after painting upon the blank darkness a sort of rehearsal whilst waking, a crowd of ladies, and perhaps a festival and dances. And I heard it said, or I said to myself, 'These are English ladies from the unhappy times of Charles I. These are the wives and daughters of those who met in peace, and sat at the same tables, and were allied by marriage, or by blood; and yet, after a certain day in August 1642, never smiled upon each other again, nor met but in the field of battle; and at Marston Moor, at Newbury, or at Naseby, cut asunder all ties of love by the cruel sabre, and washed away in blood the memory of ancient friendship.' The ladies danced, and looked as lovely as the court of George IV. DE QUINCEY.

IF there were dreams to sell
   What would you buy?
Some cost a passing bell;
   Some a light sigh
That shakes from life's fresh crown
Only a rose-leaf down.
If there were dreams to sell,
Merry and sad to tell,
And the crier rang the bell,
   What would you buy?

BEDDOES.

The offender's sorrow lends but weak relief
To him that bears the strong offence's cross.

SONN. XXXIV.

THUS use your frog: put your hook, I mean the arming wire, through his mouth, and out at his gills, and then with a fine needle and silk sew the upper part of his leg with only one stitch to the arming wire of your hook, or tie the frog's leg above the upper joint to the armed wire; and in so doing use him as though you loved him.

IZAAK WALTON.

'WHAT, she felt the while,
Must I think?
Love's so different with us men!'
He should smile:
'Dying for my sake,
White and pink!
Can't we touch these bubbles then
But they break?'

BROWNING.

APRIL 7

But I am constant as the Northern Star.

JULIUS CÆSAR iii. I.

WORDSWORTH is destined, if any poet is, to be immortal; but immortality does not necessarily mean popularity. . . . Mankind is deeply divided in its sympathies and tastes; and for a large portion of it, not merely of those who read, but of those who create and govern opinion, that which Wordsworth loved and aimed at and sought to represent will always be the object, not only of indifference, but of genuine dislike.

DEAN CHURCH.

UPON the margin of that moorish flood
Motionless as a cloud the old man stood;
That heareth not the loud winds when they call
And moveth all together, if it move at all.

WORDSWORTH.

I do not desire you to please me, I do desire you to sing.

AS YOU LIKE IT ii. 5.

THE great poet, like the original man of the Platonists, is double, possessing the further advantage of being able to drop one half at his option, and to resume it. Some of the tenderest on paper have no sympathies beyond: and some of the austerest in their intercourse with their fellow-creatures have deluged the world with tears. It is not from the rose that the bee gathers her honey, but often from the most acrid and the most bitter leaves and petals.

LANDOR.

YET half a beast is the great God Pan,
  To laugh as he sits by the river,
Making a poet out of a man:
The true Gods sigh for the cost and pain,—
For the reed which grows nevermore again
  As a reed with the reeds in the river.

MRS. BROWNING.

This carol they began that hour,
How that life was but a flower.

AS YOU LIKE IT V. 3.

SO have I seen a rose, newly springing from the clefts of its hood, and at first it was as fair as the morning, and full with the dew of heaven as a lamb's fleece; but when a ruder breath had forced upon its virgin modesty, and dismantled its too youthful and unripe retirements, it began to put on darkness and to decline to softness and the symptoms of a sickly age; it bowed the head and broke its stalk, and, at night, having lost some of its leaves and all its beauty, it fell into the portion of weeds and outworn faces.

JEREMY TAYLOR.

ALL the flowers of the spring
Meet to perfume our burying:
These have but their growing prime,
And man does flourish but his time:
Survey our progress from our birth;
We are set, we grow, we turn to earth.
Sweetest breath and clearest eye
Like perfumes go out and die;
And consequently this is done,
As shadows wait upon the sun.

WEBSTER.

A spirit I am, indeed:
But am in that dimension grossly clad,
Which from the womb I did participate.

TWELFTH NIGHT V. I.

O HEAVEN, it is mysterious, it is awful to consider that we not only carry each a future ghost within him; but are, in very deed, ghosts! Those limbs, whence had we them; this stormy force; this life-blood with its burning passion? They are dust and shadow; a shadow-system gathered round our ME; wherein through some moments or years, the divine essence is to be revealed in the flesh.

CARLYLE.

AND yet, as angels in some brighter dreams
Call to the soul when man doth sleep,
So some strange thoughts transcend our wonted themes
And into glory peep.

If a star were confined in a tomb,
Her captive flames must needs burn there;
But when the hand that locked her up gives room,
She 'll shine through all the sphere.

VAUGHAN.

Things done well,
And with a care, exempt themselves from fear.

KING HENRY VIII. i. 2.

A MAN of sensibility finds words, and a language tender, passionate, and expressive of his feelings; you imagine he paints objects and actions, while in reality he paints passion, and affects us by the image of his own imagination. . . . This animated expression is the very characteristic of great writers; but it is not by any means confined to great and important subjects; the most familiar ideas are equally capable of the tincture of sensibility.

USHER.

AND still she slept an azure-lidded sleep,
In blanched linen, smooth and lavender'd,
While he from forth the closet brought a heap
Of candied apple, quince, and plum, and gourd,
With jellies soother than the creamy curd,
And lucent syrops, tinct with cinnamon;
Manna and dates in Argosies transferr'd
From Fez; and spiced dainties, every one
From silken Samarcand to cedar'd Lebanon.
These delicates he heap'd with glowing hand
On golden dishes and in baskets bright
Of wreathed silver: sumptuous they stand
In the retired quiet of the night,
Filling the chilly room with perfume light.

KEATS.

Honour pricks me on. Yea, but how if honour prick me off when I came on? How then?

I KING HENRY IV. V. I.

I BELIEVE, an please your Honour, quoth the Corporal, that if it had not been for the quantity of brandy we set fire to every night, and the claret and cinnamon with which I plied your Honour off . . . And the geneva, Trim, added my uncle Toby, which did us more good than all . . . I verily believe, continued the Corporal, we had both, an please your Honour, left our lives in the trenches, and been buried in them too. . . . The noblest grave, Corporal, cried my uncle Toby, his eyes sparkling as he spoke, that a soldier could wish to lie down in! . . . But a pitiful death for him! an please your Honour, replied the Corporal.

STERNE.

If he that on the field is slain
Be in the bed of honour lain,
He that is beaten may be said
To lie in honour's truckle-bed.
For as we see the eclipsèd sun
By mortals is more gazed upon
Than when, adorned with all his light,
He shines in serene sky most bright,
So valour in a low estate
Is most admired and wondered at.

SAMUEL BUTLER.

Mine eyes are made the fools o' the other senses,
Or else worth all the rest.

MACBETH ii. I.

IT is also no reproach to the most finished scholar or greatest gentleman in the land that he be absolutely without eye for painting or ear for music—that in his heart he prefer the popular print to the scratch of Rembrandt's needle, or the songs of the hall to Beethoven's 'C Minor Symphony.'

Let him but have the wit to say so, and not feel the admission a proof of inferiority.

Art happens—no hovel is safe from it, no Prince may depend on it, the vastest intelligence cannot bring it about, and puny efforts to make it universal end in quaint comedy, and coarse farce.

WHISTLER.

BEAUTY itself doth of itself persuade
The eyes of men without an orator,
What needeth then apologies be made
To set forth that which is so singular?

LUCRECE.

That due of many now is thine alone:
Their images I lov'd I view in thee.

SONN. XXXI.

IN the children of noble races, trained by surrounding art, and at the same time in the practice of great deeds, there is an intense delight in the landscape of their country as *memorial*; a sense not taught to them, nor teachable to any others; but in them, innate; and the seal and reward of persistence in great national life; the obedience and the peace of ages having extended gradually the glory of the revered ancestors also to the ancestral land; until the motherhood of the dust, the mystery of the Demeter from whose bosom we came, and to whose bosom we return, surrounds and inspires, everywhere, the local awe of field and fountain.

RUSKIN.

WHERE each old poetic mountain
  Inspiration breathed around:
Every shade and hallowed fountain
  Murmured deep a solemn sound.

GRAY.

APRIL 15

Truly, sir, I am a poor fellow that would live.

MEASURE FOR MEASURE ii. 1.

HE never greatly cared for the society of what are called good people. If any of them were scandalised (and offences were sure to arise) he could not help it. When he has been remonstrated with for not making more concessions to the feelings of good people, he would retort by asking, what one point did these good people ever concede to him?

CHARLES LAMB.

AND much as Wine has played the Infidel
And robbed me of my Robe of Honour—well,
 I wonder often what the Vintners buy
One-half so precious as the stuff they sell.

Yet ah, that Spring should vanish with the Rose!
That Youth's sweet-scented Manuscript should close
 The Nightingale that in the branches sang,
Ah whence, and whither flown again, who knows?

FITZGERALD'S *Omar Khayyám.*

Show his eyes, and grieve his heart;
Come like shadows, so depart.

MACBETH iv. 1.

THE 'Epipsychidion' I cannot look at; the person whom it celebrates was a cloud instead of a Juno. . . . It is an idealised history of my life and feelings. I think one is always in love with some thing or other; the error, and I confess it is not easy for spirits cased in flesh and blood to avoid it, consists in seeking in a mortal image the likeness of what is, perhaps, eternal.

SHELLEY.

THE desire of the moth for the star,
Of the night for the morrow,
The devotion to something afar
From the sphere of our sorrow.

SHELLEY.

God help thee, shallow man! God make incision in thee!

AS YOU LIKE IT iii. 2.

BEAUTY has an expression beyond and far above the one woman's soul that it clothes, as the words of genius have a wider meaning than the thought that prompted them: it is more than a woman's love that moves us in a woman's eyes. . . . The noblest nature sees the most of this impersonal expression in beauty.

GEORGE ELIOT.

BEAUTY is not, as fond men misdeem,
An outward show of things, that only seem;
But that fair lamp, from whose celestial ray
That light proceeds which kindleth lover's fire,
Shall never be extinguished nor decay.
But when the vital spirits do expire,
Unto her native planet shall retire,
For it is heavenly born and cannot die,
Being a parcel of the purest sky.

SPENSER.

O, never say that I was false of heart,
Though absence seem'd my flame to qualify.

SONN. CIX.

WHIP me such stoics, great Governor of nature! said I to myself—Wherever thy providence shall place me for the trials of my virtue—whatever is my danger—whatever is my situation—let me feel the movements which rise out of it; and which belong to me as a man; and if I govern them as a good one, I will trust the issues to thy justice; for thou hast made us, and not we ourselves.

STERNE.

Tell me not, Sweet, I am unkind,—
  That from the nunnery
Of thy chaste breast and quiet mind
  To war and arms I fly.

True, a new mistress now I chase,
  The first foe in the field;
And with a stronger faith embrace
  A sword, a horse, a shield.

Yet this inconstancy is such
  As you, too, shall adore:
I could not love thee, dear, so much,
  Loved I not Honour more.

LOVELACE.

Pale primroses,
That die unmarried, ere they can behold
Bright Phœbus in his strength—a malady
Most incident to maids.

WINTER'S TALE iv. 4.

'THESE are for you, dear uncle,' said Clare Arundel, as she give him a rich cluster of violets. 'Just now the woods are more fragrant than the gardens, and these are the produce of our morning walk. I could have brought you some primroses, but I do not like to mix violets with anything.'

'They say primroses make a capital salad,' said Lord St. Jerome.

'Barbarian!' exclaimed Lady St. Jerome, 'I see you want luncheon; it must be ready.'

LORD BEACONSFIELD.

IN vain, through every changeful year,
  Did Nature lead him as before;
A primrose by a river's brim
A yellow primrose was to him,
  And it was nothing more.

WORDSWORTH.

Banks with pioned and twilled brims
Which spongy April at thy hest betrims
To make cold nymphs chaste crowns.

TEMPEST iv. I.

THERE was a greater variety of colours in the embroidery of the meadows, a more lively green in the leaves and grass, a brighter crystal in the streams, than what I ever met with in any other region. The light itself had something more shining and glorious in it than that of which the day is made in other places.

ADDISON.

The chilly sunset faintly told
Of unmatured green, valleys cold,
Of the green, thorny, bloomless hedge,
Of rivers green with spring-tide sedge,
Of primroses by shelter'd rills
And daisies on the aguish hills.

KEATS.

Flora,
Peering in April's front.

WINTER'S TALE iv. 4.

RAIN had fallen in the night. Here and there hung a milk-white cloud with folded sail. The south-west left it its bay of blue, and breathed below. At moments the fresh scent of herb and mould swung richly in warmth. The young beech-leaves glittered, pools of rain-water made the road-ways laugh, the grass-banks under hedges rolled their interwoven weeds in cascades of many-shaded green to right and left; a squirrel crossed ahead, a lark went up a little way to ease his heart, closing his wings when the burst was over; startled black-birds, darting with a clamour like a broken cock-crow, looped the wayside woods from hazel to oak-scrub; short flights, quick spirits everywhere, steady sunshine above.

GEORGE MEREDITH.

Now each creature joys the other
  Passing happy days and hours:
One bird reports unto another
  By the fall of silver showers;
Whilst the earth, our common Mother,
  Hath her bosom decked with flowers.

DANIEL.

Yea, this man's brow, like to a title-leaf
Foretells the nature of a tragic volume.

2 KING HENRY IV. i. I.

DANTE does not come before us as a large catholic mind; rather as a narrow and even sectarian mind: it is partly the fruit of his age and position, but partly the fruit of his own nature. His greatness has, in all senses, concentred itself into fiery emphasis and depth. He is world-great not because he is world-wide, but because he is world-deep.

CARLYLE.

THEREFORE, the loftier rose the song
To touch the secret things of God,
The deeper pierced the hate that trod
On base men's track who wrought the wrong;
Till the soul's effluence came to be
Its own exceeding agony.

D. G. ROSSETTI.

I am that I am; and they that level
At my abuses, reckon up their own.

SONN. CXXI.

THOSE who accuse Shakespeare to have wanted learning give him the greater commendation. He was naturally learned; he needed not the spectacles of books to read Nature; he looked inwards, and found her there. I cannot say he is everywhere alike; were he so, I should do him injury to compare him with the greatest of mankind. He is many times flat, insipid; his comic wit degenerating into clenches, his serious swelling into bombast. But he is always great when some great occasion is presented to him; no man can say he ever had a fit subject for his wit, and did not then raise himself as high above the rest of poets,

Quantum lenta solent inter viberna capressi.

DRYDEN.

HITHER, as to their fountain, other stars
Repairing, in their golden urns draw light.

MILTON.

Violets, dim,
But sweeter than the lids of Juno's eyes.

WINTER'S TALE iv. 4.

AND because the Breath of Flowers is far sweeter in the Air (where it comes and goes, like the Warbling of Music), than in the hand, therefore nothing is more fit for that delight, than to know, what be the Flowers, and Plants, that do best perfume the air. Roses, Damask and Red, are fast Flowers of their Smells; so that, you may walk by a whole Row of them, and find nothing of their Sweetness; yea, though it be in a Morning's Dew. Bays likewise yield no smell, as they grow. Rosemary little, nor Sweet-Marjoram. That, which above all Others, yields the sweetest Smell in the Air, is the Violet. Specially the white-double Violet, which comes twice a year; About the middle of April, and about Bartholomew-tide.

BACON.

WHITE or duskier violet,
Fair as those that in far years,
With their buds left luminous,
And their little leaves made wet
From the warmer dew of tears,
Mother's tears in extreme need,
Hid the limbs of Iamus.—

SWINBURNE.

I am never merry when I hear sweet music.

MERCHANT OF VENICE V. I.

EVEN that vulgar and Tavern-Musick, which makes one man merry, another mad, strikes in me a deep fit of Devotion, and a profound contemplation of the first composer; there is something in it of divinity more than the Ear discovers; it is a Hieroglyphical and Shadowed Lesson of the whole world, and creatures of God, such a melody to the Ear, as the whole world well understood, would afford the understanding.

SIR THOMAS BROWNE.

ORPHEUS with his lute made trees,
And the mountain-tops that freeze,
Bow themselves, when he did sing:
To his music, plants and flowers
Ever sprung; as sun and showers
There had made a lasting spring.

Everything that heard him play,
Even the billows of the sea,
Hung their heads, and then lay by.
In sweet music is such art:
Killing care and grief of heart
Fall asleep, or hearing, die.

KING HENRY VIII. iii. I.

APRIL 26

The man that hath no music in himself.

MERCHANT OF VENICE V. I.

THERE are persons who, fortunately for themselves, are so indifferent to music that they do not mind the barrel organ. It is neither better nor worse to them than the notes of Patti; and from the voice of that siren, as from all music, they withdraw their attention without difficulty.

ANDREW LANG.

Some cry up Haydn, some Mozart,
Just as the whim bites; for my part,
I do not care a farthing candle
For either of them, or for Handel.
Cannot a man live free and easy
Without admiring Pergolesi?
Or through the world with comfort go,
That never heard of Doctor Blow?

CHARLES LAMB.

And a rich fellow enough, go to; and a fellow that hath had losses; and one that hath two gowns and everything handsome about him.

MUCH ADO iv. 2.

EFFORTS have been made to obtain in English some term equivalent to *Philister* or *épicier*; Mr. Carlyle has made several such efforts: 'respectability with its thousand gigs,' he says;—well, the occupants of every one of those gigs is, Mr. Carlyle means, a Philistine. However, the word *respectable* is far too valuable a word to be thus perverted from its proper meaning: if the English are ever to have a word for the thing we are speaking of,—and so prodigious are the changes which the modern spirit is introducing, that even we English shall perhaps one day come to want such a word,—I think we had much better take the term *Philistine* itself.

MATTHEW ARNOLD.

Immediately
Was Samson as a public servant brought,
In their state livery clad; before him pipes
And timbrels, on each side went armèd guards,
Both horse and foot, before him and behind
Archers and slingers, cataphracts and spears.
At sight of him the people with a shout
Rifted the air, clamouring their god with praise,
Who had made their dreadful enemy their thrall.

MILTON.

A day in April never came so sweet,
To show how costly summer was at hand.

MERCHANT OF VENICE ii. 9.

NATURE does not like our benevolence or our learning much better than she likes our frauds and wars. When we come out of the caucus, or the bank, or the Abolition Convention, or the temperance meeting, or the Transcendental Club, into the fields and woods, she says to us, 'So hot, my little sir!'

EMERSON.

I HEARD a thousand blended notes
While in a grove I sate reclined,
In that sweet mood when pleasant thoughts
Bring sad thoughts to the mind.

To her fair works did Nature link
The human soul that in me ran;
And much it grieved my heart to think
What man has made of man.

WORDSWORTH.

Call'd Marina,
For I was born at sea.

PERICLES V. I.

I HAD not been ten minutes in the place before I fell in love with the most beautiful creature the world has ever seen. She was standing silent and majestic, in the centre of one of the rooms of the statue gallery, and the very first glimpse of her struck one breathless with the sense of her beauty. . . . She is not a clever woman evidently. I do not think she laughs or talks much,—she seems too lazy to do more than smile. She is only beautiful. This divine creature has lost her arms which have been cut off at the shoulders, but she looks none the less lovely for the accident. She may be some two-and-thirty years old, and she was born about two thousand years ago. Her name is the Venus of Milo.

THACKERAY.

LOVE still has something of the sea
From whence his mother rose;
No time his slaves from doubt can free
Nor give their thoughts repose.

SIR CHARLES SEDLEY.

When shepherds pipe on oaten straws,
And merry larks are ploughmen's clocks.

LOVE'S LABOUR'S LOST V. 2.

FOR Nature, as green as she looks, rests everywhere on dread foundations, were we farther down; and Pan, to whose music the nymphs dance, has a cry in him that can drive all men distracted.

CARLYLE.

NOR flute, nor lute, nor gittern can
So chant it as the pipe of Pan:
Cross-gartered swains and dairy girls
With faces smug and round as pearls,
When Pan's shrill pipe begins to play,
With dancing wear out night and day,
The bagpipe's drone his hum lays by,
When Pan sounds up his minstrelsy.

LYLY

MAY

Golden lads and girls all must,
As chimney-sweepers, come to dust.
CYMBELINE iv. 2.

I LIKE to meet a sweep—understand me—not a grown sweeper—old chimney-sweepers are by no means attractive—but one of those tender novices, blooming through their first nigritude, the maternal washings not quite effaced from the cheek—such as come forth with the dawn, or somewhat earlier, with their little professional notes sounding like the *peep peep* of a young sparrow; or liker to the matin lark, shall I pronounce them, in their aerial ascents not seldom anticipating the sunrise? I have a kindly yearning towards these dim specks—poor blots—innocent blacknesses—I reverence these young Africans of our own growth—these almost clergy imps, who sport their cloth without assumption. CHARLES LAMB.

Now hardly here and there a hackney-coach
Appearing, show'd the ruddy morn's approach,
Now Moll had whirl'd her mop with dextrous airs,
Prepared to scrub the entry and the stairs.
The youth with broomy stumps began to trace
The kennel's edge, where wheels had worn the place.
The small-coal man was heard with cadence deep,
Till drown'd in shriller notes of chimney-sweep.

SWIFT.

More matter for a May morning.

TWELFTH NIGHT iii. 4.

GO out, in the spring-time, among the meadows that slope from the shores of the Swiss lakes to the roots of their lower mountains. There, mingled with the taller gentians and the white narcissus, the grass grows deep and free; as you follow the winding mountain-paths, beneath arching boughs all veiled and dim with blossom,—paths that for ever droop and rise over the green banks and mounds sweeping down in scented undulation, steep to the blue water, studded here and there with new-mown heaps, filling all the air with fainter sweetness,—look up towards the higher hills, where the waves of everlasting green roll silently into their long inlets among the shadows of the pines.

RUSKIN.

THE whole earth
The beauty wore of promise, that which sets
The budding rose above the rose full-blown.

WORDSWORTH.

God give you good rest!

COMEDY OF ERRORS iv. 3.

FESTIVAL rest representeth that celestial estate whereof the very heathens themselves, which had not the means whereby to apprehend much, did notwithstanding imagine that it must needs consist in rest, and have therefore taught that above the highest movable spheres there is no thing which feeleth alteration, motion, or change; but all things immutable, unsubject to passion, blest with eternal continuance in a life of the highest perfection, and of that complete abundant sufficiency within itself which no possibility of want, maim, or defect can touch.

HOOKER.

THEN gin I think on that which Nature said,
Of that same time when no more Change shall
be,
But steadfast rest of all things, firmly stay'd
Upon the pillars of Eternity,
That is contrayr to Mutability;
For all that moveth doth in Change delight:
But thenceforth all shall rest eternally
With Him that is the God of Sabaoth hight:
Oh! that great Sabaoth God, grant me that
Sabaoth's sight!

SPENSER.

MAY 4

When wheat is green, when hawthorn buds appear.
MIDSUMMER-NIGHT'S DREAM i. I.

WE may say of angling as Dr. Boteler said of strawberries: 'Doubtless God could have made a better berry, but doubtless God never did'; and so, if I might be judge, God never did make a more calm, quiet, innocent recreation than angling.

IZAAK WALTON.

THIS day Dame Nature seemed in love,
The lusty sap began to move;
New juice did stir th' embracing vines,
And birds had drawn their valentines.
The jealous trout, that low did lie,
Rose at a well-dissembled fly:
There stood my friend, with patient skill,
Attending of his trembling quill.

WOTTON.

He must needs go that the Devil drives.

ALL'S WELL i. 3.

ON the spot where Tom Idle (for whom I have an unaffected pity) made his exit from this wicked world, and where you see the hangman smoking his pipe as he reclines on the gibbet and views the hills of Harrow or Hampstead beyond—a splendid marble arch, a vast and modern city—clean, airy, painted drab, populous with nursery-maids and children, the abodes of wealth and comfort—the elegant, the prosperous, the polite Tyburnia rises, the most respectable district in the habitable globe!

THACKERAY.

Thou wert a sinner, thou poor man!
Thou wert athirst; and didst not see
That, though we take what we desire,
We must not snatch it eagerly.

MATTHEW ARNOLD.

MAY 6

Why then comes in the sweet o' the year.

WINTER'S TALE iv. 3.

WHAT two extraordinary substances to be made, by little creatures, out of roses and lilies! What a singular and lovely energy in nature to impel these little creatures thus to fetch out the sweet and elegant properties of the coloured fragrances of the gardens, and serve them up to us for food and light,—honey to eat, and waxen tapers to eat it by!

LEIGH HUNT.

AND this was on the sixtë morn of May,
Which May had painted with his softë showers
This garden full of leavës and of flowers;
And craft of mannë's hand so curiously
Arrayèd hath this garden twewëly
That never was there garden of such price
But if it were the very Paradise.
The odour of flowers and the freshë sight
Would have made any pensive hertë light
That ever was born, but if too great sickness
Or too great sorrow held it in distress.

CHAUCER.

MAY 7

Death is a fearful thing—
And shamed life a hateful.

MEASURE FOR MEASURE iii. I.

IF the nearness of our last necessity brought a nearer conformity to it, there were a happiness in hoary hairs, and no calamity in half senses. But the long habit of living indisposes us for dying: when avarice makes us the sport of death; when even *David* grew politickly cruel, and *Solomon* could hardly be said to be the wisest of men.

SIR THOMAS BROWNE.

It is not growing like a tree
In bulk, doth make Man better be;
Or standing long an oak, three hundred year,
To fall a log at last, dry, bald, and sere:
A lily of a day
Is fairer far in May,
Although it fall and die that night—
It was the plant and flower of Light.
In small proportions we just beauties see;
And in short measures life may perfect be.

BEN JONSON.

For as the sun is daily new and old,
So is my love still telling what is told.

SONN. LXXVI.

AS Love is the son of Plenty, who was the offspring of Prudence, he is subtle, intriguing, full of stratagems and devices; as the son of Poverty, he is fawning, begging, serenading, delighting to lie at a threshold, or beneath a window. By the father, he is audacious, full of hopes, conscious of merit, and therefore quick of resentment. By the mother, he is doubtful, timorous, mean-spirited, fearful of offending, and abject in submissions.

ADDISON.

The lark now leaves his wat'ry nest,
  And climbing shakes his dewy wings,
He takes this window for the East,
  And to implore your light he sings.
Awake, awake, the morn will never rise
Till she can dress her beauty at your eyes.

DAVENANT.

Take thou my oblation, poor but free,
Which is not mix'd with seconds, knows no art,
But mutual render, only me for thee.

SONN. CXXV.

ONE knocked at the Beloved's Door; and a Voice asked from within, Who is there? and he answered, It is I. Then the Voice said, This House will not hold Me and Thee. And the Door was not opened. Then went the Lover into the Desert, and fasted and prayed in Solitude. And after a Year he returned, and knocked again at the Door. And again the Voice asked, Who is there? and he said, It is Thyself!—and the Door was opened to him.

FITZGERALD, *from the Persian.*

IF, as I have, you also do
  Virtue in woman see,
And dare love that, and say so too,
  And forget the He and She;

And if this love, though placèd so,
  From profane eyes you hide,
Which will not faith on this bestow,
  Or, if they do, deride:

Then you have done a braver thing
  Than all the Worthies did;
And a braver thence will spring,
  Which is, to keep that hid!

DONNE.

Love's not Time's fool, though rosy lips and cheeks
Within his bending sickle's compass come.

SONN. CXVI.

SURE, love *vincit omnia*; is immeasurably above all ambition, more precious than wealth, more noble than name. He knows not life that knows not that; he hath not felt the highest faculty of the soul who hath not enjoyed it. In the name of my wife I write the completion of hope, and the summit of happiness. To have such a love is the one blessing, in comparison of which all earthly joy is of no value; and to think of her is to praise God.

THACKERAY.

O LOVE, they wrong thee much
That say thy sweet is bitter,
When thy rich fruit is such
As nothing can be sweeter.
Fair house of joy and bliss,
Where truest pleasure is,
I do adore thee;
I know thee what thou art,
I serve thee with my heart,
And fall before thee.

ANON. 1605.

One good deed dying tongueless
Slaughters a thousand, waiting upon that.
Our praises are our wages.

WINTER'S TALE i. 2.

IT is a great happiness to be praised of them that are most praiseworthy.

PHILIP SIDNEY.

THERE is delight in singing, though none hear
Beside the singer; and there is delight
In praising, though the praiser sit alone
And see the praised far off him, far above.

LANDOR.

Grace is grace, despite of all controversy.

MEASURE FOR MEASURE i. 2.

ONE should be fearful of being wrong in poetry, when one thinks differently from the poets, and in religion when one thinks differently from the saints.

JOUBERT (*translated by* MATTHEW ARNOLD).

NAY, and I wonder less at God's respect
For man, a minim jot in time and space,
Than at the soaring faith of His elect,
That gift of gifts, the comfort of His grace.

ROBERT BRIDGES.

I know I love in vain, strive against hope;
Yet, in this captious and intenible sieve,
I still pour in the waters of my love,
And lack not to lose still.

ALL'S WELL i. 3.

HER high exalted sunbeams have set the phœnix-nest of my breast on fire, and myself have brought Arabian spiceries of sweet passions and praises, to furnish out the funeral flame of my folly.

NASH.

Come hither, shepherd's swain!
Sir, what do you require?
I pray thee, show to me thy name.
My name is Fond Desire.

When wert thou born, Desire?
In pomp and pride of May.
By whom, sweet boy, wert thou begot?
By Fond Conceit, men say.

E. VERE, EARL OF OXFORD.

These violent delights have violent ends,
And in their triumph die, like fire and powder.

ROMEO AND JULIET ii. 6.

TRUE, 'tis an unhappy circumstance of life, that Love should ever die before us; and that the Man should outlive the Lover. But say what you will, 'tis better to be left, than never to have been loved. To pass our youth in dull indifference, to refuse the sweets of life, because they once must leave us, is as preposterous, as to wish to have been born old, because we one day must be old. For my part, my youth may wear and waste, but it shall never rust in my possession.

CONGREVE.

LET the sweet heavens endure,
Not close and darken above me,
Before I am quite quite sure
  That there is one to love me;
Then let come what come may,
To a life that has been so sad,
  I shall have had my day.

TENNYSON.

And one man in his time plays many parts,
His acts being seven ages.

AS YOU LIKE IT ii. 7.

IN this also is the little world of man compared, and made more like the Universal (man being the measure of all things) that the four Complexions resemble the four Elements, and the seven Ages of man the seven Planets; whereof our infancy is compared to the Moon, in which we seem only to live and grow, as Plants; the second Age to Mercury, wherein we are taught and instructed; our third age to Venus, the days of Love, Desire, and Vanity; the fourth to the Sun, the strong, flourishing, and beautiful Age of man's life; the fifth to Mars, in which we seek honour and victory, and in which our thoughts travel to ambitious ends; the sixth Age is ascribed to Jupiter, in which we begin to take account of our time, judge of ourselves, and grow to the perfection of our understanding; the last and seventh Age to Saturn, wherein our days are sad and overcast, and in which we find by dear and lamentable experience, and by the loss which can never be repaired, that of all our vain passions and affections past, the sorrow only abideth. RALEIGH.

NOTHING hath got so far
But Man hath caught and kept it as his prey.
His eyes dismount the highest star;
He is in little all the sphere.
Herbs gladly cure our flesh, because that they
Find their acquaintance there.

GEORGE HERBERT.

Bare ruined choirs, where late the sweet birds sang.

SONN. LXXIII.

THERE is surely nothing better in Rome; nothing perhaps exactly so good. The grounds and gardens are immense, and the great rusty-red city wall stretches away behind them, and makes Rome seem vast without making them seem small. There is everything—dusky avenues, trimmed by the clippings of centuries, groves and dells, and glades and glowing pastures, and reedy fountains and great flowering meadows studded with enormous slanting pines. The day was delicious, the trees were all one melody, the whole place seemed a revelation of what Italy and hereditary grandeur can do together.

HENRY JAMES.

THE weary poet, thy sad son,
  Upon thy soil, under thy skies,
Saw all Italian things save one—
  Italia; this thing missed his eyes;
The old mother-might, the breast, the face,
That reared, that lit the Roman race;
This not Leopardi saw; but we,
What is it, mother, that we see,
        What, if not thee?

SWINBURNE.

Nay, it is ten times true; for truth is truth
To the end of reckoning.

MEASURE FOR MEASURE V. I.

OUR Trimmer adores the goddess Truth, though in all ages she has been scurvily used, as well as those that worshipped her. 'Tis of late become such a ruining virtue, that mankind seems to be agreed to commend and avoid it; yet the want of practice, which repeals the other laws, has no influence upon the law of truth, because it has root in Heaven, and an intrinsic value in itself that can never be impaired: She shows her greatness in this, that her enemies, even when they are successful, are ashamed to own it.

HALIFAX.

FOR want of me the world's course will not fail:
When all its work is done, the lie shall rot;
The truth is great, and shall prevail,
When none cares whether it prevail or not.

COVENTRY PATMORE.

Servile to all the skyey influences.

MEASURE FOR MEASURE iii. 1.

HERE the surface of things is certainly humdrum, the streets dingy, the green places, where the child goes a-maying, tame enough. But nowhere are things more apt to respond to the brighter weather, nowhere is there so much difference between rain and sunshine, nowhere do the clouds roll together more grandly; those quaint suburban pastorals gathering a certain quality of grandeur from the background of the great city, with its weighty atmosphere, and portent of storm in the rapid light on dome and bleached stone steeples.

WALTER PATER.

In this huge world, which roars hard by,
Be others happy if they can!
But in my helpless cradle I
Was breathed on by the rural Pan.

I on men's impious uproar hurled
Think often as I hear them rave
That peace has left the upper world
And only keeps now in the grave.

MATTHEW ARNOLD.

MAY 19

There sleeps Titania, some time of the night,
Lull'd in these flowers with dances and delight.

MIDSUMMER-NIGHT'S DREAM ii. 1.

THERE grew the four sorts of Violets, Cowslops, Melilots, Rose-parsley or Passeflower, Bluebottles, Gyth, Ladies' Seal, Vatrachium, Aquilegia, Lily Convally, Amaranth, Flower-gentle, Idessmus, all sorts of sweet pinks, and small flowering herbs of odoriferous fragrance and smell, Roses of Persia, having the smell of musk and amber, and innumerable sorts of others without setting, but naturally growing in a wonderful distribution, peeping out from between their green leaves, and barbs very delightful to behold.

Eng. Trans. of 'Hypnerotomachia.'

It was a chosen plot of fertile land,
Amongst wide waves set, like a little nest,
As if it had by Nature's cunning hand
Been choicely picked out from all the rest,
And laid forth for ensample of the best:
No dainty flower or herb that grows on ground,
No arboret with painted blossoms drest
And smelling sweet, but there it might be found
To bud out fair, and throw her sweet smells all
around.

SPENSER.

There's not the smallest orb which thou behold'st
But in his motion like an angel sings.

MERCHANT OF VENICE V. I.

IN his loneliness and fixedness he yearneth towards the journeying moon, and the stars that still sojourn, yet still move onward; and everywhere the blue sky belongs to them, and is their appointed rest, and their native country, and their own natural homes, which they enter unannounced, as lords that are certainly expected, and yet there is a silent joy at their arrival.

COLERIDGE.

Soon as the evening shades prevail
The moon takes up the wondrous tale;
And nightly, to the listening earth,
Repeats the story of her birth:
Whilst all the stars that round her burn,
And all the planets, in their turn,
Confirm the tidings as they roll,
And spread the truth from pole to pole.

ADDISON.

Let me not to the marriage of true minds
Admit impediments.

SONN. CXVI.

'NEVER mind, Sammy,' replied Mr. Weller, 'it'll be a wery agonisin' trial to me at my time of life, but I'm pretty tough, that's vun consolation, as the wery old turkey remarked wen the farmer said he should be obliged to kill him for the London market.'

'What'll be a trial?' inquired Sam.

'To see you married, Sammy—to see you a dilluded wictim, and thinkin' in your innocence that it's all wery capital,' replied Mr. Weller. 'It's a dreadful trial to a father's feelin's, that ere, Sammy.'

DICKENS.

CROWN'D with flowers I saw fair Amaryllis
 By Thyrsis sit, hard by a fount of Chrystal,
And with her hand more white than snow or lilies,
 On sand she wrote *My faith shall be immortal:*
And suddenly a storm of wind and weather
Blew all her faith and sand away together.

ANON. 1611.

Truly, shepherd, in respect of itself it is a good life; but in respect that it is a shepherd's life, it is naught.

AS YOU LIKE IT iii. 2.

ABOUT six or seven o'clock I walk out into a common that lies hard by the house, where a great many young wenches keep sheep and cows, and sit in the shade singing of ballads. I go to them and compare their voices and beauties to some ancient shepherdesses that I have read of, and find a vast difference there; but trust me, I think these are as innocent as those could be. I talk to them, and find they want nothing to make them the happiest people in the world but the knowledge that they are so. Most commonly, when we are in the midst of our discourse, one looks about her, and spies her cows going into the corn, and then away they all run as if they had wings at their heels.

DOROTHY OSBORNE.

As one who long in populous city pent,
Where houses thick and sewers annoy the air,
Forth issuing on a summer's morn, to breathe
Among the pleasant villages and farms
Adjoin'd, from each thing met conceives delight;
The smell of grain, or tedded grass, or kine,
Or dairy, each rural sight, each rural sound;
If chance, with nymph-like step, fair virgin pass,
What pleasing seem'd, for her now pleases more;
She most, and in her look sums all delight.

MILTON.

MAY 23

Could beauty have better commerce than with honesty?

HAMLET iii. I.

IN Beauty, that of Favour, is more than that of Colour; and that of Decent and Gracious Motion, more than that of Favour. That is the best part of Beauty, which a picture cannot express; no, nor the first Sight of the Life. There is no Excellent Beauty, that hath not some Strangeness in the Proportion.

BACON.

BEAUTY, unto me divine,
Makes my honest thoughts incline
Unto better things than that
Which the vulgar aimeth at.
And I vow I grieve to see
Any fair and false to be;
Or when I sweet pleasures find
Match'd with a defilèd mind.

WITHER.

Truth hath a quiet breast.

KING RICHARD II. i. 3.

IN troubled Water you can scarce see your Face, or see it very little, till the Water be quiet and stand still. So in troubled times you can see little Truth; when times are quiet and settled, Truth appears.

SELDEN.

GENTLE times for love are meant;
Who for parting pleasure strain
Gather roses in the rain,
Wet themselves, and lose their scent.

MARVELL.

Truly, sir, and pleasure will be paid, one time or another.

TWELFTH NIGHT ii. 4.

PLEASURE seizes the whole man who addicts himself to it, and will not give him leisure for any good office in life which contradicts the gaiety of the present hour. You may indeed observe in people of pleasure a certain complacency and absence of all severity, which the habit of a loose and unconcerned life gives them; but tell the man of pleasure your secret wants, cares, or sorrows, and you will find that he has given up the delicacy of his passions to the craving of his appetites. STEELE.

Who is the honest man?
He that doth still, and strongly, good pursue;
To God, his neighbour, and himself most true.
Whom neither force nor fawning can
Unpin, or wrench from giving all their due.

Who never melts or thaws
At close temptations. When the day is done
His goodness sets not, but in dark can run.
The sun to others writeth laws
And is their virtue. Virtue is his sun.

GEORGE HERBERT.

I say, there is no darkness but ignorance.

TWELFTH NIGHT iv. 2.

I KNOW no disease of the soul but ignorance; not of the arts and sciences, but of itself: yet relating to those it is a pernicious evil, the darkener of man's life, the disturber of his reason, and the common confounder of truth; with which a man goes groping in the dark, no otherwise than if he were blind. Great understandings are most racked and troubled with it; nay, sometimes they will rather choose to die than not to know the things they study for.

BEN JONSON.

O SUCH a life as he resolved to live,
When he had learned it,
When he had gathered all books had to give!
Sooner, he spurned it.

BROWNING.

Whose youth and freshness
Wrinkles Apollo's, and makes stale the morning.

TROIL. AND CRESS. ii. 2.

THE very beautiful rarely love at all. Those precious images are placed above the reach of the Passions. Time alone is permitted to efface them; Time, the father of the Gods, and even *their* consumer.

LANDOR.

WAS this the face that launched a thousand ships,
And burnt the topless towers of Ilium?
Sweet Helen, make me immortal with a kiss.
Her lips suck forth my soul! see where it flies;
Come, Helen, come, give me my soul again!

MARLOWE.

The front of heaven was full of fiery shapes,
Of burning cressets.

I KING HENRY IV. iii. I.

IT had been wild weather when I left Rome, and all across the Campagna the clouds were sweeping in sulphurous blue, with a clap of thunder or two, and breaking gleams of sun along the Claudian aqueduct, lighting up the infinity of its arches like the bridge of Chaos. But as I climbed the long slope of the Alban Mount, the storm swept finally to the north, and the noble outline of the domes of Albano, and graceful darkness of its ilex-grove, rose against pure streaks of alternate blue and amber: the upper sky gradually flushing through the last fragments of rain-cloud in deep, palpitating azure, half æther and half dew.

RUSKIN.

As the dissolving warmth of dawn may fold
A half unfrozen dew-globe, green, and gold,
And crystalline, till it becomes a wingèd mist,
And wanders up the vault of the blue day,
Outlives the noon, and on the sun's last ray
Hangs o'er the sea, a fleece of fire and amethyst.

SHELLEY.

The heavens themselves, the planets and this
centre,
Observe degree, priority, and place,
Insisture, course, proportion, season, form,
Office, and custom, in all line of order.

TROIL. AND CRESS. i. 3.

THE reason why first we do admire those things which are greatest, and second those things which are ancientest, is because the one are least distant from the infinite substance, the other from the infinite continuance, of God.

HOOKER.

STERN lawgiver! yet thou dost wear
The Godhead's most benignant grace;
Nor know we anything so fair
As is the smile upon thy face:
Flowers laugh before thee on their beds,
And fragrance in thy footing treads;
Thou dost preserve the stars from wrong;
And the most ancient Heavens, through thee, are
fresh and strong.

WORDSWORTH.

It will be short: the interim is mine;
And a man's life's no more than to say, One.

HAMLET V. 2.

'THE blind bow-boy,' who smiles upon us from the end of terraces in old Dutch gardens, laughingly hails his bird-bolts among a fleeting generation. But for as fast as ever he shoots, the game dissolves and disappears into eternity from under his falling arrows; this one is gone ere he is struck; the other has but time to make one gesture and give one passionate cry; and they are all the things of a moment.

LOUIS STEVENSON.

O LOVE me, then, and now begin it,
Let us not lose the present minute:
For time and age will work that rack
Which time nor age shall ne'er call back.

CAREW.

Kissing with golden face the meadows green,
Gilding pale streams with heavenly alchemy.

SONN. XXXIII.

THEN comes another such corner of woodland, rocky, strewn with stones curiously notched and veined; and here, too, infinite summer hills open and recede and melt into further and nearer forms in solid undulation without change, billows of the inland crowned not with foam but with grass, and clothed with trees, not moulded out of mutable water.

SWINBURNE.

CHRIST keep the Hollow Land
All the summer-tide!
Still we cannot understand
How the waters glide,

Only dimly seeing them
Coldly slipping through
Many green-lipped cavern-mouths
Where the hills are blue.

WILLIAM MORRIS.

JUNE

O, when mine eyes did see Olivia first,
Methought she purg'd the air of pestilence.

TWELFTH NIGHT i. 1.

I KNOW a very pretty instance of a little girl of whom her father was very fond, who once, when he was in a melancholy fit and had gone to bed, persuaded him to rise in good humour by saying, 'My dear papa, please to get up and let me help you on with your clothes, that I may learn to do it when you are an old man.

BOSWELL.

Nor quality nor reputation
Forbid me yet my flame to tell,
Dear five-years-old befriends my passion,
And I may write till she can spell.

For while she makes her silkworms' beds
With all the tender things I swear;
Whilst all the house my passion reads
In papers round her baby's hair;

She may receive and own my flame,
For though the strictest prudes should know it,
She'll pass for a most virtuous dame,
And I for an unhappy poet.

PRIOR.

And Adam was a gardener.
And what of that?

2 KING HENRY VI. iv. 2.

GOD Almighty first planted a Garden. And indeed it is the Purest of Humane pleasures. It is the Greatest Refreshment to the Spirits of Man; without which, Buildings and Palaces are but Gross Handiworks: And a Man shall ever see, that when Ages grow to Civility and Elegancy, Men come to Build Stately, sooner than to Garden Finely: as if Gardening were the Greater Perfection.

BACON.

Such was that happy Garden-state
While man there walked without a mate:
After a place so pure and sweet,
What other help could yet be meet!
But 'twas beyond a mortal's share
To wander solitary there:
Two paradises 'twere in one,
To live in Paradise alone.

MARVELL.

We that are true lovers run into strange capers.

AS YOU LIKE IT ii. 4.

AFTER all, Love's Sectaries are a 'reason unto themselves.' We have gone retrograde in the noble Heresy since the days when Sidney proselyted our nation to this mixed health and disease: the kindliest symptom yet the most alarming crisis in the ticklish state of youth; the nourisher and the destroyer of hopeful wits; the mother of twin-births, wisdom and folly, valour and weakness; the servitude above freedom; the gentle mind's religion; the liberal superstition.

CHARLES LAMB.

HE or she that hopes to gain
Love's best fruit without some pain
Hopes in vain.

Cupid's livery no one wears
But must put on hopes and fears,
Smiles and tears.

ANON.

JUNE 4

There's rosemary, that's for remembrance; pray, love, remember: and there is pansies, that's for thoughts.

HAMLET iv. 5.

THE noble mansion is most distinguished by the beautiful images it retains of beings passed away; and so is the noble mind.

LANDOR.

LILIES for a bridal bed—
Roses for a matron's head—
Violets for a maiden dead—
  Pansies let my flowers be.

SHELLEY.

O me, what eyes hath love put in my head,
Which have no correspondence with true sight!

SONN. CXLVIII.

A CERTAIN institution in Mr. Podsnap's mind, which he called 'the Young Person,' may be considered to have been embodied in his daughter. It was an inconvenient and exacting institution, as requiring everything in the world to be filed down and fitted to it. The question about everything was, would it bring a blush to the cheek of the young person? and the inconvenience of the young person was, that according to Mr. Podsnap, she seemed to be always liable to burst into blushes where there was no need at all. There appeared to be no line of demarcation between the young person's excessive innocence, and another person's guiltiest knowledge.

DICKENS.

But in my country, where I most desire—
In Ecron, Gaza, Asdod, and in Gath—
I shall be named among the famousest
Of women, sung at solemn festivals,
Living and dead recorded.

MILTON.

But are you flesh and blood?
Have you a working pulse? and are no fairy-motion?

PERICLES V. I.

IN a little shabby, chilly corridor adjoining is a fresco of Lionardo, a Virgin and child, with the *Donatorio.* It is very small, simple, and faded, but has all the artist's magic. It has that mocking, illusive refinement, that hint of a vague *arrière-pensée,* which marks every stroke of Lionardo's brush. Is it the perfection of irony or the perfection of tenderness? What does he mean, what does he affirm, what does he deny? Magic would not be magic if we could explain it.

HENRY JAMES.

HER face is like the milky way i' the sky,
A meeting of gentle lights without a name.

SUCKLING.

I may speak of thee as the traveller doth of Venice:
'Venetia, Venetia,
Chi non ti vede non ti pretia.'

LOVE'S LABOUR'S LOST iv. 2.

TO take a boat in a pleasant evening, and with music to row upon the waters, which Plutarch so much applauds, Ælian admires, upon the river Peneus, in those Thessalian fields beset with green bays, where birds so sweetly sing, that passengers, enchanted as it were with their heavenly music, *omnium laborum et curarum obliviscantur,* forget forthwith all labours, cares, and grief; or in a gundilo through the grand canale in Venice, to see those goodly palaces, must needs refresh and give content to a melancholy dull spirit.

BURTON.

HUSH! in the canal below
Don't you hear the plash of oars
Underneath the lantern's glow,
And a thrilling voice begins
To the sound of mandolins?—
Begins singing of amore
And delire and dolore—
O the ravishing tenore!

THACKERAY.

JUNE 8

Since brass, nor stone, nor earth, nor boundless sea,
But sad mortality o'ersways their power—

SONN. LXV.

OUT of monuments, names, words, proverbs, traditions, private records and evidences, fragments of stories, passages of books, and the like, we do save and recover somewhat from the deluge of Time.

BACON.

O YE who patiently explore
The wreck of Herculanean lore,
What rapture! could ye seize
Some Theban fragment, or unroll
One precious, tender-hearted scroll
Of pure Simonides.

WORDSWORTH.

JUNE 9

Well, whiles I am a beggar I will rail
And say there is no sin but to be rich.

KING JOHN ii. 1.

VAST power and possessions make a man shamefully afraid of dying; and I am convinced that many of the most intrepid adventurers who, being poor, enjoy the full use of their natural energies, would, if at the very instant of going into action news were brought to them that they had unexpectedly succeeded to an estate in England of £50,000 a year, feel their dislike to bullets furiously sharpened, and their efforts at self-possession proportionally difficult.

DE QUINCEY.

EXTOL not riches, then, the toil of fools,
The wise man's cumbrance, if not snare; more apt
To slacken virtue, and abate her edge,
Than prompt her to do aught may merit praise.

MILTON.

Not of a woman's tenderness to be,
Requires nor child nor woman's face to see.

CORIOLANUS V. 3.

TRULY it is to be noted, that children's plays are not sports, and should be noted as their most serious actions.

FLORIO'S *Montaigne.*

HERE on this lawn thy boys and girls shall run
And ply their gambols when their tasks are done;
There from that window shall their mother view
The happy tribe, and smile at all they do;
While thou, more gravely, hiding thy delight,
Shall cry, 'O childish!' and enjoy the sight.

CRABBE.

For all the world like cutler's poetry
Upon a knife, 'Love me, and leave me not.'

MERCHANT OF VENICE V. I.

'OH,' cried Anne eagerly, 'I hope I do justice to all that is felt by you, and by those that resemble you. I should deserve utter contempt if I dared to suppose that true attachment and constancy were known only by woman. . . . All the privilege I claim for my own sex (it is not a very enviable one; you need not covet it) is that of loving longest, when existence or when hope is gone.

JANE AUSTEN.

'THE morn is merry June, I trow,
The rose is budding fain;
But she shall bloom in winter snow
Ere we two meet again.'
He turn'd his charger as he spake,
Upon the river-shore,
He gave the bridle-reins a shake,
Said 'Adieu for evermore,
My love!
And adieu for evermore.'

SCOTT.

Ah! yet doth beauty, like a dial hand,
Steal from his figure, and no pace perceived.

SONN. CIV.

WHAT a dead thing is a clock, with its ponderous embowelments of lead and brass, its pert or solemn dulness of communication, compared with the simple altar-like structure and silent heart-language of the old dial! It stood as the garden-god of Christian gardens. Why is it almost everywhere vanished? If its business-use be superseded by more elaborate inventions, its moral uses, its beauty, might have pleaded for its continuance. It spoke of moderate labours, of pleasures not protracted after sunset, of temperance and good hours. It was the primitive clock, the horologe of the first world. Adam could scarce have missed it in Paradise.

CHARLES LAMB.

Except our loves at this noon stay
We shall new shadows make the other way.
As the first were made to blind
Others, these which come behind
Will work upon ourselves, and blind our eyes,
If our loves faint, and westwardly decline,
To me thou falsely thine,
And I to thee mine actions shall disguise.
The morning shadows wear away,
But these grow longer all the day;
But, oh! love's day is short, if love decay.

DONNE.

JUNE 13

The west yet glimmers with some streaks of day.

MACBETH iii. 3.

THROUGH the tall openings of the stair-cased streets, up which, here and there, the cattle were going home slowly from the pastures below, the Alban heights, between the great walls of the ancient houses, seemed close upon him,—a vaporous screen of dun violet against the setting sun, with those waves of surpassing grace in their boundary-line characteristic of volcanic hills. The coolness of the little brown market-place, for the sake of which even the working people were leaving the plain, in long file, through the olive-gardens, to pass the night, was grateful after the heats of Rome.

WALTER PATER.

WHEN the grey-hooded Even,
Like a sad votarist in palmer's weed,
Rose from the hindmost wheels of Phœbus' wain.

MILTON.

uch is the simplicity of man to hearken after the flesh.

LOVE'S LABOUR'S LOST i. 1.

TO most men argument makes the point in hand more doubtful and considerably less impressive. After all, man is not a reasoning animal, he is a eeing, feeling, contemplating, acting animal.

CARDINAL NEWMAN.

O FRIVOLOUS mind of man,
Light ignorance, and hurrying, unsure thoughts!
Though man bewails you not,
How *I* bewail you!

MATTHEW ARNOLD.

Softly and swiftly, sir, for the priest is ready.

TAMING OF THE SHREW, V. I.

TO Church in the morning, and there saw a wedding in the Church, which I have not seen for many a day; and the young people so merry one with another, and strange to see what delight we married people have to see these poor fools decoyed into our condition, every man and woman gazing and smiling at them.

PEPYS.

THE golden gates of sleep unbar
  Where Strength and Beauty met together,
Kindle their image like a star
  In a sea of glassy weather.
Night, with all thy stars, look down,—
  Darkness, weep thy holiest dew,—
Never smiled the inconstant moon
          On a pair so true.

SHELLEY.

Where great patricians shall attend, and shrug,
I' the end, admire.

CORIOLANUS i. 9.

YESTERDAY Colonel and Mrs. Crawley entertained a select party at dinner at their house in Mayfair. Their excellencies the Prince and Princess of Peterwaradin, H. E. Papoosh Pasha, the Turkish Ambassador (attended by Kibob Bey, Dragoman of the Mission), the Marquis of Steyne, Earl of Southdown, Sir Pitt and Lady Jane Crawley, Mr. Wagg, etc. After dinner Mrs. Crawley had an assembly, which was attended by the Duchess (Dowager) of Stilton, Duc de la Gruyère, Marchioness of Cheshire, Marchese Alexandro Strachino, Comte de la Brie, Baron Schapzuger, Chevalier Tosti, Countess of Slingstone and Lady F. Macadam, Major-General and Lady G. Macbeth and (2) Miss Macbeths; Viscount Paddington, Sir Horace Fogey, Hon. Sands Bedwin, Bobbachy Bahawder, and an etc. which the reader may fill at his pleasure through a dozen close lines of small type.

THACKERAY.

O THAT I too, I, now were
By deep cells and waterfloods,
Streams of ancient hills, and where
All the wan green places bear
Blossoms cleaving to the sod,
Fruitless fruit, and grasses fair,
Or such darkest ivy-buds
As divide thy yellow hair,
Bacchus.—

SWINBURNE.

JUNE 17

Beauty's pattern to succeeding men.

SONN. XIX.

'SIR, ancient sculpture is the true school of modesty. But where the Greeks had modesty we have cant; where they had poetry, we have cant; where they had patriotism, we have cant; where they had anything that exalts, delights, or adorns humanity, we have nothing but cant, cant, cant.'

PEACOCK.

OF all God's works which do this world adorn,
There is no one more fair and excellent
Than is man's body both for power and form
While it is kept in sober government,
But none than it more foul and indecent
Distempered through misrule and passions base.

SPENSER.

The summer's flower is to the summer sweet,
Though to itself it only live and die.

SONN. XCIV.

THERE is in every human countenance either a history or a prophecy, which must sadden, or at least soften, every reflecting observer.

COLERIDGE.

Go, lovely Rose,
Tell her that wastes her time and me,
That now she knows
When I resemble her to thee,
How sweet and fair she seems to be.

Tell her that's young,
And shuns to have her graces spied,
That hadst thou sprung
In deserts where no men abide,
Thou must have uncommended died.

WALLER.

But in a fiction, in a dream of passion.

HAMLET ii. 2.

THE true tears are those which are called forth by the *beauty* of poetry; there must be as much admiration in them as sorrow.

CHATEAUBRIAND (*trans. by* M. ARNOLD).

'Tis better in a play
Be Agamemnon, than himself indeed.
How oft with danger of the field beset,
Or with home-mutinies, would he un-be
Himself; or, over cruel altars weeping,
Wish, that with putting off a vizard he
Might his true inward sorrow lay aside!
The shows of things are better than themselves.

ANON. (*Tragedy of Nero*).

The fair, the chaste, and unexpressive she.

AS YOU LIKE IT iii. 2.

NOR blame it, readers, in those years to propose to themselves such a reward, as the noblest dispositions above other things in this life have sometimes preferred; whereof not to be sensible, when good and fair in one person meet, argues both a gross and shallow judgment, and withal an ungentle and swainish breast.

MILTON.

A FACE that should content me wondrous well
Should not be fair, but lovely to behold;
Of lively looks, all grief for to repel
With right good grace, so would I that it should
Speak without words, such words as none can tell;
Her tress should also be of crispèd gold.
With wit, and these, perchance, I might be tried,
And knit again with knot that should not slide.

WYAT.

JUNE 21

Now stand you on the top of happy hours.

SONN. XVI.

THOSE marble busts of the Emperors, they seemed as if they were to stand for ever, as they had stood from the living days of Rome, in that old marble hall, and I to partake of their permanency. Eternity was, while I thought not of Time. But he thought of me; and they are toppled down, and corn covers the spot of the noble old dwelling and its princely gardens. I feel like a grasshopper that, chirping about the grounds, escaped his scythe only by my littleness.

CHARLES LAMB.

THE dear sun floods the land
as the morning falls towards noon,
And a little wind is awake
in the best of the latter June.
They are busy winning the hay,
and the life and the picture they make,
If I were as once I was,
I should deem it made for my sake;
For here, if one need not work,
is a place for happy rest,
While one's thought wends over the world
north, south, and east, and west.

WILLIAM MORRIS.

How could communities,
Degrees in schools, and brotherhoods in cities,
Prerogative of age, crowns, sceptres, laurels,
But by degree, stand in authentic place?

TROIL. AND CRESS. i. 3.

THE best argument why Oxford should have precedence of Cambridge, is the Act of Parliament, by which Oxford is made a Body, made what it is, and Cambridge is made what it is; and in the Act it takes Place. Besides Oxford has the best monuments to show.

SELDEN.

AND that sweet city with her dreaming spires,
She needs not June for beauty's heightening.

MATTHEW ARNOLD.

A true knight;
Not yet mature, yet matchless.

TROIL. AND CRESS. iv. 5.

ON each side of a bright river he saw rise a line of brighter palaces, arched and pillared, and inlaid with deep red porphyry, and with serpentine; along the quays before their gates were riding troops of knights, noble in face and form, dazzling in crest and shield; horse and man one labyrinth of quaint colour and gleaming light—the purple, and silver, and scarlet fringes flowing over the strong limbs and clashing mail like sea-waves over rocks at sunset.

RUSKIN.

But such a knightly sightë treuëly
As was on him, was nought, withouten fail,
To look on Mars, that God is of bataile.
So like a man of armës and a knight,
He was to sen, fulfilled of high prowess;
For both he had a body, and a might
To don that thing, as well as hardiness;
And ek to sen him in his gear him dress,
So fresh, so young, so weldy seemèd he,
It was an heaven upon him for to see.

CHAUCER.

Who shall be true to us,
When we are so unsecret to ourselves?

TROIL. AND CRESS. iii. 2.

SOME have felt that these blundering lives are due to the inconvenient indefiniteness with which the Supreme Power has fashioned the natures of women; if there were one level of feminine incompetence as strict as the ability to count three and no more, the social lot of women might be treated with scientific certitude. Meanwhile the indefiniteness remains, and the limits of variation are really much wider than any one would imagine from the sameness of women's coiffure and the favourite love-stories in prose and verse.

GEORGE ELIOT.

HAVE women nursed some dream since Helen sailed
Over the sea of blood the blushing star,
That Beauty, whom frail man as Goddess hailed
When not possessing her (for such is he!),
Might in a wondering season seen afar,
  Be tamed to say not 'I', but 'we'?

GEORGE MEREDITH.

We, ignorant of ourselves,
Beg often our own harms, which the wise powers
Deny us for our good.

ANT. AND CLEOP. ii. I.

I AM apt to think that, in the day of Judgment, there will be small allowance given to the wise for their want of morals, nor to the ignorant for their want of faith, because both are without excuse. This renders the advantages equal of ignorance and knowledge. But some scruples in the wise, and some vices in the ignorant, will perhaps be forgiven upon the strength of temptation to each.

SWIFT.

WHEN wishes only weak the heart surprise,
Heaven, in its mercy, the fond prayer denies;
But when our wishes are both base and weak,
Heaven, in its justice, gives us what we seek.

CRABBE.

Full many a glorious morning have I seen
Flatter the mountain-tops with sovran eye.

SONN. XXXIII.

'FOR a man who conducts himself well,' repeated Mrs. Micawber with her clearest business manner, 'and is industrious. Precisely. It is evident to me that Australia is the legitimate sphere of action for Mr. Micawber!'

Shall I ever forget how, in a moment, he was the most sanguine of men, looking on to fortune; or how Mrs. Micawber presently discoursed about the habits of the kangaroo! Shall I ever recall the street of Canterbury on a market-day, without recalling him, as he walked back with us; expressing, in the hardy, roving manner he assumed the unsettled habits of a temporary sojourner in the land; and looking at the bullocks, as they came by, with the eye of an Australian farmer!

DICKENS.

THE lopped tree in time may grow again,
  Most naked plants renew both fruit and flower!
The sorriest wight may find release of pain,
  The driest soil suck in some moistening shower;
Time goes by turns, and chances change by course,
From foul to fair, from better hap to worse.

SOUTHWELL.

Gives not the hawthorn bush a sweeter shade
To shepherds, looking on their silly sheep,
Than doth a rich embroider'd canopy?

3 KING HENRY VI. ii. 5.

THERE were hills which garnished their proud heights with stately trees: humble valleys, whose base estate seemed comforted with the refreshment of silver rivers; meadows enamelled with all sorts of eye-pleasing flowers: thickets, which being lined with most pleasant shade were intressed so too by the cheerful disposition of many well-tuned birds: each pasture stored with sheep, feeding with sober security, while the pretty lambs with bleating outcry craved the dam's comfort: here a shepherd's boy piping, as though he should never be old: there a young shepherdess knitting, and withal singing; and it seemed that her voice comforted her hands, so to work, and her hands kept time to her voice-music. PHILIP SIDNEY.

IN some Arcadian valley deep withdrawn
The shepherd to the shepherd called at dawn;
Clear rang his cry; the music that it had
High on the hill awoke the Oread,
And she her sister, and afar on high
The silver echoes made divine reply,
While he, exultant, hung half startled thus,
And heard Cyllene answer Maenalus.

J. W. MACKAIL.

JUNE 28

O, my love, my love is young!

THE PASSIONATE PILGRIM.

HE had landed on an island of the still-vexed Bermoothes. . . . Hark, how Ariel sang overhead! What splendour in the heavens! What marvels of beauty about his enchanted head! And, oh you wonder! Fair Flame, by whose light the glories of being are now first seen. . . . Radiant Miranda, Prince Ferdinand is at your feet.

Or is it Adam, his rib taken from his side in sleep, and thus transformed, to make him behold his Paradise, and lose it?

GEORGE MEREDITH.

O MISTRESS mine, where are you roaming?
O, stay and hear; your true-love's coming,
That can sing both high and low:
Trip no further, pretty sweeting;
Journeys end in lover's meeting,
Every wise man's son doth know.

TWELFTH NIGHT ii. 3.

This most excellent canopy, the air, look you, this brave o'erhanging firmament, this majestical roof fretted with golden fire—

HAMLET ii. 2.

THAT stifled hum of Midnight, when Traffic has lain down to rest; and the chariot-wheels of Vanity, still rolling here and there through distant streets, are bearing her to Halls roofed-in, and lighted to the due pitch for her; and only Vice and Misery, to prowl or to moan like night-birds, are abroad: that hum, I say, like the stertorous, unquiet slumber of sick Life, is heard in Heaven! Oh, under that hideous coverlet of vapours and putrefactions and unimaginable gases, what a Fermenting-Vat lies simmering and hid! The joyful and the sorrowful are there; men are dying there, men are being born; men are praying,—on the other side of a brick partition, men are cursing; and around them is the vast, void night. CARLYLE.

UPON a trancèd summer night
Those green-robed senators of mighty woods,
Tall oaks, branch-charmèd by the earnest stars,
Dream, and so dream all night without a stir,
Save for one gradual solitary gust
Which comes upon the silence, and dies off,
As if the ebbing air had but one wave.

KEATS.

Now is he for the numbers that Petrarch flowed in.

ROMEO AND JULIET ii. 4.

FURTHERMORE, Laura may not have understood the etherealities of Petrarch. It is possible that less homage may have had a greater effect upon her: and it is highly probable (as Petrarch, though he speaks well of her natural talents, says she had not been well educated) that she had that instinctive misgiving of the fine qualities attributed to her, which is produced, even in the vainest of women, by flights to which they are unaccustomed. LEIGH HUNT.

THAT noble flame, which my breast keeps alive,
Shall still survive
When my soul 's fled.
Nor shall my love die, when my body's dead;
That shall wait on me to the lower shade,
And never fade;
My very ashes in their urn
Shall, like a hallowed lamp, for ever burn.

CAREW.

JULY

Being enthralled as I am, it will also be the bondage of certain ribbons and gloves.

WINTER'S TALE iv. 4.

MAN only can be aware of the insensibility of man to a new gown. It would be mortifying to the feelings of many ladies could they be made to understand how little the heart of man is affected by what is costly or new in their attire; how little it is biassed by the texture of their muslin, and how unsusceptible of peculiar tenderness towards the spotted, the sprigged, the mull, or the jackonet. Woman is fine for her own satisfaction alone. No man will admire her the more, no woman will like her the better for it. Neatness and fashion are enough for the former, and a something of shabbiness or impropriety will be most endearing to the latter.

JANE AUSTEN.

But who is this? what thing of sea or land?
Female of sex it seems,
That so bedeck'd, ornate, and gay,
Comes this way sailing
Like a stately ship
Of Tarsus, bound for th' isles
Of Javan or Gadire,
With all her bravery on, and tackle trim,
Sails fill'd, and streamers waving.

MILTON.

Sleep shall neither night nor day
Hang upon his pent-house lid;
He shall live a man forbid.

MACBETH i. 3.

'THEN it was that Jupiter formed the design of creating Sleep; and he added him to the number of the gods, and gave him the charge over night and rest, putting into his hands the keys of human eyes. With his own hands he mingled the juices wherewith Sleep should soothe the hearts of mortals—herb of Enjoyment and herb of Safety, gathered from a grove in Heaven; and, from the meadows of Acheron, the herb of Death; expressing from it one single drop only, no bigger than a tear that one might hide.'

WALTER PATER.

SLEEP, sleep on! forget thy pain;
  My hand is on thy brow.
My spirit on thy brain;
My pity on thy heart, poor friend;
  And from my fingers flow
The powers of life, and like a sign,
  Seal thee from thine hour of woe;
And brood on thee, but may not blend with thine.

SHELLEY.

Audacious without impudency, learned without opinion, and strange without heresy.

LOVE'S LABOUR'S LOST V. I.

THOSE have not only depraved understandings, but diseased affections, which cannot enjoy a Singularity without a Heresy, or be the Author of an Opinion without they be of a Sect also; this was the villany of the first Schism of *Lucifer*, who was not content to err alone, but drew into his Faction many Legions of Spirits, and upon this experience he tempted only *Eve*, as well understanding the communicable nature of Sin, and that to deceive but one, was tacitly and upon consequence to delude them both.

SIR THOMAS BROWNE.

THENCE up he flew, and on the Tree of Life,
The middle tree and highest there that grew,
Sat like a cormorant; yet not true life
Thereby regained, but sat devising death
To them who lived; nor on the virtue thought
Of that life-giving plant, but only used
For prospect, what well used had been the pledge
Of immortality.

MILTON.

JULY 4

Thou art a blessed fellow to think as every man thinks: never a man's thought in the world keeps the road-way better than thine.

2 KING HENRY IV ii. 2.

MESEEMETH all several, strange, and particular fashions proceed rather of folly or ambitious affectation, than of true reason: and that a wise man ought inwardly to retire his mind from the common press, and hold the same liberty and power to judge freely of all things, but for outward matters he ought absolutely to follow the fashions and form customarily received.

FLORIO's *Montaigne.*

You might have been enough the man you are,
With striving less to be so: lesser had been
The thwartings of your dispositions, if
You had not show'd them how ye were disposed
Ere they lack'd power to cross you.

CORIOLANUS iii. 2.

Of many faces, eyes and hearts,
To have the touches dearest prized.

AS YOU LIKE IT iii. 2.

THENCE to the Duke's playhouse, and saw 'Macbeth.' The King and Court there; and we sat just under them, and my Lady Castlemaine, and close to a woman that comes into the pit, a kind of a loose gossip, that pretends to be like her, and is so something. And my wife, by my troth, appeared, I think, as pretty as any of them; I never thought so much before. The King and Duke of York minded me, and smiled upon me, at the handsome woman near me.

PEPYS.

Give Beauty all her right!
She 's not to one form tied;
Each shape yields fair delight
Where her perfections bide:
Helen, I grant, might pleasing be,
And Ros'mond was as sweet as she.

CAMPION

JULY 6

Making no summer of another's green.

SONN. LXVIII.

O THE difference of divers men in the tenderness of their consciences; some are scarce touched with a wound, whilst others are wounded with a touch therein.

FULLER.

In judging others we can see too well
Their grievous fall, but not how grieved they fell;
Judging ourselves, we to our minds recall
Not how we fell, but how we grieved to fall.

CRABBE.

JULY 7

Stones whose rates are either rich or poor
As fancy values them.

MEASURE FOR MEASURE ii. 2.

THE Oriental opinion of the wholesome operation of precious stones, in that they move the mind with admirable beauties, remains perhaps at this day a part of the marvellous estimation of inert gems amongst us. Those indestructible elect bodies, as stars, shining to us out of the dim mass of matter, are comfortable to our fluxuous feeble souls and bodies: in this sense all gems are cordial, and of an influence religious. These elemental flowering lights almost persuade us of a serene eternity, and are of things (for the inestimable purity) which separate us from the superfluous study of the world.

C. M. DOUGHTY.

In his house heap pearl like pebble-stones,
Receive them free and sell them by the weight,
Bags of fiery opals, sapphires, amethysts,
Jacinths, hard topaz, grass-green emeralds,
Beauteous rubies, sparkling diamonds,
And seld-seen costly stones of so great price,
As one of them, indifferently rated,
And of a caract of this quality,
May serve in peril of calamity
To ransom great kings from captivity.

MARLOWE.

Night's candles are burnt out, and jocund day
Stands tiptoe on the misty mountain-tops.

ROMEO AND JULIET iii. 5.

THE sea, the atmosphere, the light, bore each an orchestral part in this universal lull. Moonlight, and the first timid tremblings of the dawn, were by this time blending; and the blendings were brought into a still more exquisite state of unity by a slight silvery mist, motionless and dreamy, that covered the woods and fields, but with a veil of equable transparency. Except the feet of our own horses, which, running on a sandy margin of the road, made but little disturbance, there was no sound abroad. In the clouds, and on the earth, prevailed the same majestic peace.

DE QUINCEY.

I WITH the morning's love have oft made sport,
And, like a forester, the groves may tread,
Even till the eastern gate, all fiery red,
Opening on Neptune with fair blessed beams
Turns into yellow gold his salt green streams.

MIDSUMMER-NIGHT'S DREAM iii. 2.

Is this thy body's end?

SONN. CXLVI.

THIS regard to his meals and repose makes Succus order all the rest of his time with relation to them. He will undertake no business that may hurry his spirits, or break in upon his hours of eating and rest. If he reads, it shall be only for half an hour, because that is sufficient to amuse the spirits; and he will read something that may make him laugh, as rendering the body fitter for its food and rest. Or if he has, at any time, a mind to indulge a grave thought, he always has recourse to a useful treatise upon the ancient cookery. Succus is an enemy to all party matters, having made it an observation that there is as good eating amongst the Whigs as amongst the Tories.

LAW.

ALAS, the shorté throat, the tender mouth,
Maketh that East and West, and North and South,
In earth, in air, in water, men to swink
To get a glutton dainty meat and drink.

CHAUCER.

There was a star danced, and under that was I born.

MUCH ADO ii. 1.

IN short, I was that which we graver people call a hoyting girl; but to be just to myself, I never did mischief to myself or people, nor one immodest word or action in my life, though skipping and activity was my delight, but upon my mother's death, I then began to reflect, and, as an offering to her memory, I flung away those little childnesses that had formerly possessed me, and by my father's command, took upon me charge of his house and family, which I so ordered by my excellent mother's example as found acceptance in his sight. I was very well beloved by all our relations and my mother's friends, whom I paid a great respect to, and I ever was ambitious to keep the best company, which I have done, I thank God, all the days of my life.

LADY FANSHAWE.

If I freely may discover
What would please me in my lover,
I would have her fair and witty,
Savouring more of court than city;
A little proud, but full of pity.

BEN JONSON.

JULY 11

The setting sun, and music at the close.

KING RICHARD II. ii. I.

THEN Sir Bedivere cried, Ah, my Lord Arthur, what shall become of me now ye go from me, and leave me here alone among mine enemies? Comfort thyself, said the King, and do as well as thou mayest, for in me is no trust to trust in. For I will into the Vale of Avilion, to heal me of my grievous wound. And if thou hear never more of me, pray for my soul. But ever the queens and the ladies wept and shrieked that it was pity to hear. And as soon as Sir Bedivere had lost sight of the barge, he wept and wailed, and so took the forest.

MALLORY.

WHEN some surpassing spirit
Whose light adorned the world around it, leaves
Those who remain behind, nor sobs nor groans,
The passionate tumult of a clinging hope;
But pale despair and cold tranquillity,
Nature's vast frame, the web of human things,
Birth and the grave, that are not as they were.

SHELLEY.

For every man has business and desire,
Such as it is; and for mine own poor part,
Look you, I'll go pray.

HAMLET i. 5.

THE only happy people in the world are the good man, the sage, and the saint; but the saint is happier than either of the others, so much is man by his nature formed for sanctity.

JOUBERT (*translated by* MATTHEW ARNOLD).

WHAT loud uproar bursts from the door!
The wedding guests are there;
But in the garden-bower the bride
And bridesmaids singing are;
And hark, the little vesper-bell
Which biddeth me to prayer!

COLERIDGE.

If the dull substance of my flesh were thought—

SONN. XLIV.

THE earth of the Sistine Adam that begins to burn; the woman-embodied burst of Adoration from his sleep; the twelve great torrents of the spirit of God that pause above us there, urned in their vessels of clay; the waiting in the shadow of futurity of those through whom the Promise and Presence of God went down from the Eve to the Mary . . . not only these, not only the troops of terror torn up from the earth by the four-quartered winds of the Judgment, but every fragment and atom of stone that he ever touched became instantly inhabited by what makes the hair stand up and the words be few.

RUSKIN.

His heart was as the heart of his own land,
  And at his feet as natural servants lay
  Twilight and dawn and night and labouring day.

He was most awful of the sons of God,
  Even now men seeing seemed at his lips to see
  The trumpet of the judgment that should be,
And in his right hand terror for a rod,
  And in the breath that made the mountains bow
  The horned fire of Moses on his brow.

SWINBURNE.

O, widow Dido! ay, widow Dido.

TEMPEST ii. I.

WHEN evils press sore upon me, and there is no retreat from them in this world, then I take a new course,—I leave it—and as I have a clearer idea of the Elysian fields than I have of heaven, I force myself, like Eneas, into them—I see him meet the pensive shade of his forsaken Dido—and wish to recognise it—I see the injured spirit wave her head and turn off silent from the author of her miseries and dishonours,—I lose the feelings for myself in hers—and in those affections which were wont to make me mourn for her when I was at school.

STERNE.

STILL fly, plunge deeper in the bowering wood!
  Averse, as Dido did with gesture stern
  From her false friend's approach in Hades turn,
Wave us away, and keep thy solitude!

MATTHEW ARNOLD.

Yet better thus, and known to be contemn'd,
Than still contemn'd and flatter'd.

KING LEAR iv. I.

BUT to live to fourscore years, and be found dancing among the idle virgins! to have had near a century of allotted time, and then to be called away from the giddy notes of a Mayfair fiddle! to have to yield your roses too, and then drop out of the bony clutch of your old fingers a wreath that came from a Parisian band-box!

THACKERAY.

SEE how the World its Veterans rewards!
A Youth of Frolics, an old Age of Cards;
Fair to no purpose, artful to no end,
Young without Lovers, old without a Friend;
A Fop their Passion, but their Prize a Sot;
Alive, ridiculous, and dead, forgot!

POPE.

Following darkness like a dream.

MIDSUMMER-NIGHT'S DREAM V. 2.

AND now, not Puck alone, but the whole state of fairies, had gone to inevitable wreck and destruction, had not a timely apparition interposed, at whose boldness Time was astounded; for he came not with the habit or the forces of a deity, who alone might cope with Time, but as a simple mortal, clad as you might see a forester that hunts after wild conies by the cold moonshine; or a stalker of stray deer, stealthy and bold. But by the golden lustre in his eye, and the passionate wanness in his cheek, and by the fair and ample space of his forehead, which seemed a palace framed for the habitation of all glorious thoughts, he knew that this was his great rival, who had power given him to rescue whatsoever victims Time should clutch, and to cause them to live for ever in his immortal verse. CHARLES LAMB.

THE revelling elves, at noon of night,
  Shall throng no more beneath thy boughs
When moonbeams shed a solemn light
  And every star intensely glows.

TENNYSON.

And humming water must o'erwhelm thy corpse
Lying with simple shells.

PERICLES iii. I.

AND first there were but three men in her, and in a moment she capsized, and there were but two; and again she was struck by a vast mass of water, and there was but one; and again she was thrown bottom upward, and that one, with his arm struck through the broken planks, and waving as if for the help that could never reach him, went down into the deep.

DICKENS.

FULL fathom five thy father lies;
Of his bones are coral made;
Those are pearls that were his eyes:
Nothing of him that doth fade
But doth suffer a sea-change
Into something rich and strange.

TEMPEST i. 2.

I grant I never saw a goddess go;
My mistress, when she walks, treads on the ground.

SONN. CXXX.

THERE are faces which nature charges with a meaning and pathos not belonging to the single human soul that flutters beneath them, but speaking the joys and sorrows of foregone generations—eyes that tell of deep love which doubtless has been and is somewhere, but not paired with these eyes—perhaps paired with pale eyes that can say nothing; just as a national language may be instinct with poetry unfelt by the lips that use it.

GEORGE ELIOT.

NAY, love, you did give all I asked, I think—
More than I merit, yes, by many times.
But had you—oh, with the same perfect brow,
And perfect eyes, and more than perfect mouth,
And the low voice my soul hears, as a bird
The fowler's pipe, and follows to the snare—
Had you, with these the same, but brought a mind!
Some women do so.

BROWNING.

We must be patient: but I cannot choose but weep, to think they should lay him i' the cold ground.

HAMLET iv. 5.

WHEN nature had performed what she would, grace stept forth, and took our child from nature, and gave it such gifts over and above the power of nature, as where it could not creep in earth by nature it was straightway well able to go to heaven by grace. It could not then speak by nature, and now it doth praise God by grace; it could not then comfort the sick and careful mother by nature, and now through prayer it is able to help father and mother by grace; and yet, thanked be nature, that hath done all she could do, and grace that hath done more and better than we would wish she should have done. Peradventure yet you do wish that nature had kept it from death a little longer, yea, but grace hath carried it where now no sickness can follow, nor any death hereafter meddle with it; and instead of a short life with troubles on earth, it doth now live a life that never shall end with all manner of joy in heaven.

ASCHAM.

THY mother's treasure wert thou; alas! no longer
To visit her heart with wondrous joy; to be
Thy father's pride; ah, he
Must gather his faith together, and his strength make stronger.

ROBERT BRIDGES.

Some that will evermore peep through their eyes
And laugh like parrots at a bag-piper.

MERCHANT OF VENICE i. 1.

THE rest of the morning was easily whiled away in dawdling through the green-house, where the loss of her favourite plants, unwarily exposed, and nipped by the lingering frost, raised the laughter of Charlotte,—and in visiting her poultry-yard, where, in the disappointed hopes of her dairy-maid, by hens forsaking their nests, or being stolen by a fox, or in the rapid decease of a promising young brood, she found fresh sources of merriment.

JANE AUSTEN.

How brave lives he that keeps a fool,
Although the rate be deeper;
But he that is his own fool, sir,
Does live a great deal cheaper.

FLETCHER.

And my large kingdom for a little grave,
A little little grave, an obscure grave.

KING RICHARD II. iii. 3.

I HAD rather sleep in the southern corner of a little country churchyard than in the tomb of the Capulets.

BURKE.

THE garlands wither on your brow,
  Then boast no more your mighty deeds;
Upon Death's purple altar now
  See where the Victor-victim bleeds:
        Your heads must come
        To the cold tomb;
Only the actions of the just
Smell sweet and blossom in the dust.

SHIRLEY.

Not marble, nor the gilded monuments
Of princes, shall outlive this powerful rhyme.

SONN. LV.

LET us consider, too, how differently young and old are affected by the words of some Classic author, such as Homer or Horace. Passages which to a boy are but rhetorical commonplaces, neither better nor worse than a hundred others which any clever writer might supply; which he gets by heart, and thinks very fine, and imitates, as he thinks, successfully, in his own flowing versification, at length come home to him, when long years have passed, and he has had experience of life, and pierce him as if he had never before known them, with their sad earnestness and vivid exactness. Then he comes to understand how it is that lines, the birth of some chance morning or evening at an Ionian festival, or among the Sabine hills, have lasted generation after generation, for thousands of years, with a power over the mind, and a charm, which the current literature of his own day, with all its obvious advantages, is utterly unable to rival.

CARDINAL NEWMAN.

BUT wise words taught in numbers for to run
Recorded by the Muses, live for aye;
Ne may with storming showers be washt away,
Ne bitter-breathing winds with harmful blast,
Nor age, nor envy, shall them ever waste.

SPENSER.

For what he has he gives, what thinks he shows;
Yet gives he not till judgment guide his bounty.

TROIL. AND CRESS. iv. 5.

SO that, if we had not very rich, we generally had very happy, friends about us; for this remark will hold good through life, that the poorer the guest, the better pleased he ever is with being treated: and as some men gaze with admiration at the colours of a tulip, or the wing of a butterfly, so I was by nature an admirer of happy human faces. However, when any one of our relations was found to be a person of very bad character, a troublesome guest, or one we desired to get rid of, upon his leaving my house I ever took care to lend him a riding-coat, or a pair of boots, or sometimes a horse of small value, and I always had the satisfaction of finding he never came back to return them.

GOLDSMITH.

TRUE is it, that we have seen better days,
And have with holy bell been knoll'd to church
And sat at good men's feasts and wiped our
eyes
Of drops that sacred pity hath engender'd:
And therefore sit you down in gentleness
And take upon command what help we have
That to your wanting may be minister'd.

AS YOU LIKE IT ii. 7.

Offer pure incense to so pure a shrine.

LUCRECE.

HE had before this time received some rebukes from Jones, who always expressed great bitterness against any misbehaviour to the fair part of the species, who, if considered, he said, as they ought to be, in the light of dearest friends, were to be cultivated, honoured, and caressed with the utmost love and tenderness: but, if regarded as enemies, were a conquest, of which a man ought rather to be ashamed than to value himself upon it.

FIELDING.

WHEN I had done what man could do,
And thought the place mine own,
The enemy lay quiet too,
And smil'd at all was done.

I sent to know from whence, and where
These hopes and this relief?
A spy inform'd, Honour was there,
And did command in chief.

March, march (quoth I), the word straight give,
Let's lose no time, but leave her,
That Giant upon air will live,
And hold it out for ever.

SUCKLING.

The oath of a lover is no stronger than the word of a tapster; they are both the confirmer of false reckonings.

AS YOU LIKE IT iii. 4.

IT had ever, as I told the reader, been one of the singular blessings of my life, to be almost every hour of it miserably in love with some one; and my last flame happening to be blown out by a whiff of jealousy on the sudden turn of a corner, I had lighted it afresh at the pure taper of Eliza but about three months before—swearing as I did it, that it should last me through the whole journey—why should I dissemble the matter? I had sworn to her eternal fidelity.

STERNE.

TAKE, O take those lips away,
  That so sweetly were forsworn;
And those eyes, the break of day,
  Lights that do mislead the morn:
But my kisses bring again, bring again;
Seals of love, but sealed in vain, sealed in vain.

MEASURE FOR MEASURE iv. 1.

She holds her virtue still, and I my mind.

CYMBELINE i. 4.

I TOOK her hand in mine, and we went out of the ruined place; and as the morning mists had risen long ago, when I first left the forge, so the evening mists were rising now; and in all the broad expanse of tranquil light they showed to me, I saw no shadow of another parting from her.

DICKENS.

DEAR, if you change, I 'll never choose again;
Sweet, if you shrink, I 'll never think of love;
Fair, if you fail, I 'll judge all beauty vain;
Wise, if too weak, more wits I 'll never prove;
Dear, sweet, fair, wise! change, shrink, nor be
not weak,
And, on my faith, my faith shall never break.

ANON.

My bonds in thee are all determinate,
For how do I hold thee but by thy granting?

SONN. LXXXVII.

SO when Sir Launcelot was departed, the Queen made no manner of sorrow in showing, to none of his blood, nor to none other: but, wit ye well, inwardly, as the book saith, she took great thought, but she bare it out with a proud countenance, as though she felt nothing nor danger.

MALLORY.

SINCE there 's no help, come, let us kiss and part!
  Nay, I have done. You get no more of me.
And I am glad, yea, glad with all my heart,
  That thus so clearly I myself can free.
Shake hands for ever, cancel all our vows,
  And when we meet at any time again
Be it not seen in either of our brows
  That we one jot of former love retain.

Now at the last gasp of Love's latest breath,
  When, his pulse failing, Passion speechless lies,
When Faith is kneeling by his bed of death,
  And Innocence is closing up his eyes:
Now, if thou wouldst, when all have given him
    over,
From death to life thou mightst him yet recover!

DRAYTON.

Who chooseth me must give and hazard all he hath.

MERCHANT OF VENICE ii. 7

DESTINY is no artist. The facts that confront us are relentless. No statement of the case is adequate which maintains, by ever so delicate an implication, that in the long run and somehow it is well in temporal things with the just, and ill with the unjust. Until we have fairly looked in the face the grim truth that temporal rewards and punishments do not follow the possession or the want of spiritual or moral virtue, so long we are still ignorant what that enigma is, which speculative men, from the author of the book of Job downwards, have striven to resolve.

JOHN MORLEY.

So Virtue, given for lost,
Depressed and overthrown, as seemed,
Like that self-begotten bird
In the Arabian woods embost,
That no second knows nor third,
And lay erewhile a holocaust,
From out her ashy womb now teemed,
Revives, reflourishes, then vigorous most
When most inactive deemed;
And though her body die, her fame survives,
A secular bird, ages of lives.

MILTON.

A pageant truly play'd,
Between the pale complexion of true love
And the red glow of scorn and proud disdain.
AS YOU LIKE IT iii. 4.

AY, ay, suffer your cruelty to ruin the object of your power, to destroy your Lover—And then how vain, how lost a thing you 'll be! Nay, 'tis true: you are no longer handsome when you 've lost your Lover; your beauty dies upon the instant: For beauty is the Lover's gift; 'tis he bestows your charms—your Glass is all a cheat. The ugly and the old, whom the looking-glass mortifies, yet after commendation can be flattered by it, and discover beauties in it: For that reflects our praises, rather than your Face. CONGREVE.

THAT killing power is none of thine,
I gave it to thy voice and eyes;
Thy sweets, thy graces all are mine;
Thou art my star, shin'st in my skies:
Then dart not from thy borrowed sphere
Lightning on him that fixed thee there.

Tempt me with such affrights no more,
Lest what I made I uncreate;
Let fools thy mystic forms adore,
I 'll know thee in thy mortal state;
Wise poets that wrapt Truth in tales
Knew her themselves through all her veils.

CAREW.

Before, a joy proposed; behind, a dream.

SONN. CXXIX.

THE presence that thus so strangely rose beside the waters is expressive of what in the ways of a thousand years man had come to desire. Hers is the head upon which all 'the ends of the world are come,' and the eyelids are a little weary. It is a beauty wrought out from within upon the flesh, the deposit, little cell by cell, of strange thoughts and fantastic reveries and exquisite passions. Set it for a moment by the side of one of those white Greek goddesses or beautiful women of antiquity, and how would they be troubled by this beauty, into which the soul with all its maladies has passed!

WALTER PATER.

•

BEWARE of her fair hair, for she excels
All women in the magic of her locks;
And when she winds them round a young
man's neck,
She will not ever set him free again.

SHELLEY (*from* GOETHE).

How silver-sweet sound lovers' tongues by night.

ROMEO AND JULIET ii. 2.

ONE would think they hoped to conquer their mistresses' hearts as people tame hawks and eagles, by keeping them awake, or breaking their sleep when they are falling into it.

STEELE.

'WHO is it that this dark night
Underneath my window plaineth?'
It is one who from thy sight
Being, ah, exiled, disdaineth
Every other vulgar light.

'Why, alas, and are you he?
Be not yet these fancies changèd?'
Dear, when you find change in me,
Though from me you be estrangèd,
Let my change to ruin be.

PHILIP SIDNEY.

AUGUST

AUGUST I

Yet he that can endure
To follow with allegiance a fall'n lord
Does conquer him that did his master conquer,
And earns a place i' the story.

ANT. AND CLEOP. iii. 13.

AND certainly there cannot be two more *Fortunate* Properties; than to have a little of the Fool; and not too much of the Honest. Therefore Extreme Lovers of their Country, or Masters, were never Fortunate, neither can they be. For when a man placeth his thoughts without Himself, he goeth not his own Way.

BACON.

THAT sir which serves and seeks for gain,
  And follows but for form,
Will pack when it begins to rain,
  And leave thee in the storm.
But I will tarry; the fool will stay,
  And let the wise man fly:
The knave turns fool that runs away;
  The foo no knave, perdy.

KING LEAR ii. 4.

O you gods!
Why do you make us love your goodly gifts
And snatch them straight away? We here below
Recall not what we give, and therein may
Use honour with you. PERICLES ii. I.

TO sum up, therefore, all that can be said of his outward frame and disposition, we must truly conclude, that it was a very handsome and well-furnished lodging prepared for the reception of that prince, who in the administration of all excellent virtues reigned there a while, till he was called back to the palace of the universal emperor.

MRS. HUTCHINSON.

HE that hath found some fledged bird's nest, may
know
At first sight, if the bird be flown;
But what fair well or grove he sings in now
That is to him unknown.

VAUGHAN.

Man, proud man,
Most ignorant of what he's most assured,
His glassy essence.

MEASURE FOR MEASURE ii. 2.

THAT thinking without language is a dangerous habit. . . . Could we live with ourselves letting our animal do our thinking for us legibly? We live with ourselves agreeably so long as his projects are phrased in his primitive tongue, even though we have clearly apprehended what he means, and though we sufficiently well understand the whither of our destination under his guidance. No counsel can be saner than that the heart should be bidden to speak out in plain verbal speech within us.

GEORGE MEREDITH.

WE seek to know the moving of each sphere,
  And the strange course of th' ebbs and flows
    of Nile;
But of that clock, which in our breasts we bear,
  The subtle motions we forget the while.

We that acquaint ourselves with every zone,
  And pass the tropics and behold each pole,
When we come home are to ourselves unknown,
  And unacquainted still with our own soul.

SIR JOHN DAVIES.

AUGUST 4

A shadow like an angel, with bright hair.

KING RICHARD III. i. 4.

EACH poet gives us what he has, and what he can offer; you spread before us fairy bread, and enchanted wine; and shall we turn away with a sneer, because, out of all the multitudes of singers, one is spiritual and strange, one has seen Artemis unveiled? One, like Anchises, has been beloved of the goddess, and his eyes, when he looks on the common world of common men, are, like the eyes of Anchises, blind with excess of light. Let Shelley sing of what he saw, what none saw but Shelley!

ANDREW LANG.

Music, when soft voices die,
Vibrates in the memory;
Odours, when sweet violets sicken,
Live within the sense they quicken;

Rose-leaves, when the rose is dead,
Are heaped for the belovèd's bed;
And so thy thoughts, when thou art gone,
Love itself shall slumber on.

SHELLEY.

A jest's prosperity lies in the ear
Of him that hears it, never in the tongue
Of him that makes it.

LOVE'S LABOUR 'S LOST V. 2.

THERE is a sort of rude familiarity, which some people, by practising it among their intimates, have introduced into their general conversation, and would have it pass for innocent freedom or humour, which is a dangerous experiment in our northern climate, where all the little decorum and politeness we have are purely forced by art, and are so ready to lapse into barbarity.

SWIFT.

WHERE none were sad, and few were dull,
And each one said his best,
And beauty was most beautiful
With vanity at rest.
No taunt or scoff obscured the wit
That there rejoiced to reign;
They never could have laughed at it
If it had carried pain.

LORD HOUGHTON.

AUGUST 6

We two, that with so many thousand sighs
Did buy each other, must poorly sell ourselves
With the rude brevity and discharge of one.

TROIL. AND CRESS. iv. 4.

FLORA, always tall, had grown to be very broad too, and short of breath; but that was not much. Flora, whom he had left a lily, had become a peony; but that was not much. Flora, who had seemed enchanting in all she said and thought, was diffuse and silly: that was much. Flora, who had been spoiled and artless long ago, was determined to be spoiled and artless now: that was a fatal blow.

DICKENS.

A LITTLE while a little love
May yet be ours who have not said
The word it makes our eyes afraid
To know that each is thinking of.
Not yet the end: be our lips dumb
In smiles a little season yet:
I'll tell thee, when the end is come,
How we may best forget.

D. G. ROSSETTI.

AUGUST 7

If England to itself do rest but true.

KING JOHN V. 7.

SO I keep looking at her, and thinking of her; and as often as I consider how history is a series of waves, coming gradually to a head and then breaking, and that, as the successive waves come up, one nation is seen at the top of this wave, and then another of the next, I ask myself, counting all the waves which have come up with England at the top of them: When the great wave which is now mounting has come up, will she be at the top of it? *Illa nihil, nec me quærentem vana moratur!*—

Yes, we arraign her; but she,
The weary Titan, with deaf
Ears, and labour-dimmed eyes,
Regarding neither to right
Nor left, goes passively by,
Staggering on to her goal;
Bearing on shoulders immense,
Atlantéan, the load,
Wellnigh not to be borne,
Of the too vast orb of her fate.

MATTHEW ARNOLD.

O reason not the need: our basest beggars
Are in the poorest thing superfluous.

KING LEAR ii. 4.

WHEN you have pared away all the vanity, what solid and natural contentment does there remain which may not be had with five hundred pounds a year? Not so many servants or horses, but a few good ones, which will do all the business as well; not so many choice dishes at every meal, but at several meals all of them, which makes them both the more healthy and the more pleasant; not so rich garments nor so frequent changes, but as warm and as comely, and so frequent change, too, as is every jot as good for the master, though not for the tailor or valet-de-chambre; not such a stately palace, nor gilt rooms, nor the costlier sorts of tapestry, but a convenient brick house, with decent wainscot and pretty forest-work hangings. • COWLEY.

WEALTH'S wasteful tricks I will not learn,
Nor ape the glittering upstart fool;—
Shall not carved tables serve my turn,
But *all* must be of buhl?
Give grasping pomp its double share,—
I ask but *one* recumbent chair.

HOLMES.

To find the mind's construction in the face.

MACBETH i. 4.

ASK the married man, who has been so but for a short space of time, if those blue eyes where, during so many years of anxious courtship, truth, sweetness, serenity, seemed to be written in characters which could not be misunderstood—ask him if the characters which they now convey be exactly the same?—if for truth he does not *read* a dull virtue (the mimic of constancy) which changes not, only because it wants the judgment to make a preference?—if for sweetness he does not *read* a stupid habit of looking pleased at everything;—if for serenity he does not *read* animal tranquillity, the dead pool of the heart, which no breeze of passion can stir into health? Alas! what is this book of the countenance good for, which, when we have read so long, and thought that we understood its contents, there comes a countless list of heart-breaking errata at the end?

CHARLES LAMB.

A SWEET attractive kind of grace,
A full assurance given by looks,
Continual comfort in a face,
The lineaments of gospel books,
I trow that countenance cannot lie
Whose thoughts are legible in the eye.

MATTHEW ROYDON.

What custom wills, in all things should we do't,
The dust on antique time would lie unswept.

CORIOLANUS ii. 3.

TO burn always with this hard, gemlike flame, to maintain this ecstasy, is success in life. In a sense it might even be said that our failure is to form habits: for, after all, habit is relative to a stereotyped world, and meantime it is only the roughness of the eye that makes any two persons, things, situations, seem alike.

WALTER PATER.

WHO makes the last a pattern for next year
Turns no new leaf, but still the same thing reads;
Seen things he sees again, heard things doth hear,
And makes his life but like a pair of beads.

DONNE.

Sure, he that made us with such large discourse,
Looking before and after, gave us not
That capability and godlike reason
To fust in us unused.

HAMLET iv. 4.

I FELL also to think, what advantage these innocent animals had of man, who as soon as nature cast them into the world, find their meat dressed, the cloth laid, and the table covered; they find their drink brewed, and the buttery open, their beds made, and their clothes ready; and though man hath the faculty of reason to make him a compensation for the want of those advantages, yet this reason brings with it a thousand perturbations of mind and perplexities of spirit, griping cares and anguishes of thought, which those harmless silly creatures were exempted from.

HOWEL.

More than we
Is the least flower whose life returns,
Least weed renascent in the sea.

We are vexed and cumbered in earth's sight
With wants, with many memories;
These see their mother what she is,
Glad-growing, till August leave more bright
The apple-coloured cranberries.

SWINBURNE.

A great while ago the world begun,
With hey, ho, the wind and the rain.

TWELFTH NIGHT V. I.

NOR can it touch but of arrogant ignorance, to hold this or that nation barbarous, these or those times gross, considering how this manifold creature man, wheresoever he stand in the world, hath always some disposition of worth, entertains and affects that order of society which is best for his use, and is eminent for some one thing or other that fits his humour and the times.

DANIEL.

Some foreign writers, some our own despise ;
The ancients only or the modern prize.
Thus wit, like faith, by each man is applied
To one small sect, and all are damn'd beside.
Meanly they seek the blessing to confine,
And force that sun but on a part to shine,
Which not alone the southern wit sublimes,
But ripens spirits in cold northern climes.

POPE.

The protractive trials of great Jove
To find persistive constancy in man.

TROIL. AND CRESS. i. 3.

WHOEVER is resolved to excel in painting, or indeed in any other art, must bring all his mind to bear upon that one object, from the moment he rises till he goes to bed; the effect of every object that meets the painter's eye may give him a lesson, provided his mind is calm, unembarrassed with other objects, and open to instruction. This general attention, with other studies connected with the art, which must employ the artist in his closet, will be found sufficient to fill up life, if it was much longer than it is.

SIR JOSHUA REYNOLDS.

PAINTING is welcome.
The painting is almost the natural man;
For since dishonour traffics with man's nature,
He is but outside: these pencill'd figures are
Even such as they give out. I like your work.

TIMON i. 1.

For charity itself fulfils the law,
And who can sever love from charity?

LOVE'S LABOUR'S LOST IV. 3.

IT is by the finest tints and most insensible gradations that Nature descends from the fairest face about St. James's to the sootiest complexion in Africa. At which tint of these is it, that the ties of blood are to cease? and how many shades must we descend lower still in the scale, ere mercy is to vanish with them?

STERNE.

Root pity in thy heart, that when it grows
Thy pity may deserve to pitied be.
If thou dost seek to have what thou dost hide,
By self-example mayst thou be denied!

SONN. CXLII.

An we might have a good woman born but one every blazing star, or at an earthquake, 'twould mend the lottery well.

ALL'S WELL i. 3.

I SUPPOSE there is not a single man, or woman, who has not more or less need of that stoical resignation which is often a hidden heroism, or who, in considering his or her past history, is not aware that it has been cruelly affected by the ignorant or selfish action of some fellow-being in a more or less close relation of life. And to my mind, there can be no stronger motive than this perception, to an energetic effort, that the lives of others shall not suffer in a like manner from us.

GEORGE ELIOT.

Ah, wasteful woman! She who may
On her sweet self set her own price,
Knowing he cannot choose but pay—
How has she cheapened Paradise!
How given for nought her priceless gift,
How spoiled the bread and spilled the wine,
Which, spent with due respective thrift,
Had made brutes men, and men divine.

COVENTRY PATMORE.

Dian in her orb,
As chaste as is the bud ere it be blown.

MUCH ADO iv. I.

THE moon reigns glorious, glad of the gale; as glad as if she gave herself to its fierce caress with love.

CHARLOTTE BRONTË.

Queen and Huntress, chaste and fair,
Now the sun is laid to sleep,
Seated in thy silver chair
State in wonted manner keep:
Hesperus entreats thy light,
Goddess excellently bright.

Lay thy bow of pearl apart•
And thy crystal-shining quiver;
Give unto the flying hart
Space to breathe, how short soever;
Thou that mak'st a day of night,
Goddess excellently bright!

BEN JONSON.

AUGUST 17

How irksome is this music to my heart!

2 KING HENRY VI. ii. I.

IF you love music, hear it; go to operas, concerts, and pay fiddlers to play to you: but I insist on your neither piping or fiddling yourself. It puts a gentleman in a very frivolous, contemptible light; brings him into a great deal of bad company, and takes up a great deal of time which might be much better employed. Few things would mortify me more than to see you bearing part in a concert with a fiddle under your chin or a pipe in your mouth.

LORD CHESTERFIELD.

Thus long ago,
Ere heaving bellows learned to blow,
While organs yet were mute,
Timotheus, to his breathing flute
And sounding lyre,
Could swell the soul to rage.—

DRYDEN.

For the apparel oft proclaims the man.

HAMLET i. 3.

A GENTLEMAN in our late civil wars, when his quarters were beaten up by the enemy, was taken prisoner, and lost his life afterwards, only by staying to put on a band and adjust his periwig. He would escape like a person of quality, or not at all, and died the noble martyr of ceremony and gentility.

COWLEY.

And what art thou, thou idol ceremony?
What kind of god art thou, that suffer'st more
Of mortal griefs than do thy worshippers?
What are thy rents? what are thy comings in?
O ceremony, show me but thy worth!

KING HENRY V. iv. 1.

Your rye-straw hats put on
And these fresh nymphs encounter every one
In country footing. TEMPEST iv. 1.

THE sister of the youth, who had stolen her voice from heaven, sang alternately with her brother;—'twas a Gascon roundelay.

Viva la joia!
Fidon la tristessa!

The nymphs joined in unison, and their swains an octave below them.

Viva la joia was on her lips; *viva la joia* was in her eyes. A transient spark of amity shot across the space between us. She looked amiable;—why could I not live and end my days thus? Just Dispenser of our joys and sorrows, cried I, why could not a man sit down in the lap of content here,—and dance, and sing, and say his prayers, and go to Heaven with his nut-brown maid? Capriciously did she bend her head on one side, and dance up insidious. Then 'tis time to dance off, quoth I. STERNE.

Shake off your heavy trance!
And leap into a dance
Such as no mortals use to tread!
Fit only for Apollo
To play to, for the moon to lead
And all the stars to follow.

F. BEAUMONT.

Violated vows
'Twixt the souls of friend and friend.

AS YOU LIKE IT iii. 2.

OF the gradual abatement of kindness between friends, the beginning is often scarcely discernible by themselves, and the process is continued by petty provocations, and incivilities sometimes peevishly returned, and sometimes contemptuously neglected, which would escape all attention but that of pride, and drop from any memory but that of resentment.

DR. JOHNSON.

THEY parted—ne'er to meet again!
But never either found another
To free the hollow heart from paining—
They stood aloof, the scars remaining,
Like cliffs which had been rent asunder;
A dreary sea now flows between;
But neither heat, nor frost, nor thunder,
Shall wholly do away, I ween,
The marks of that which once hath been.

COLERIDGE.

AUGUST 21

Our thoughts are ours, their ends none of our own.

HAMLET iii. 2.

SHAKESPEARE created 'Hamlet' with his mind running on Montaigne, and placed its action and its hero in Montaigne's atmosphere and world. What is that world? It is the world of man viewed as a being *ondoyant et divers*, balancing and indeterminate, the plaything of cross motives and shifting impulses, swayed by a thousand subtle influences, physiological and pathological. Certainly the action and the hero of the original Hamlet story are not such as to compel the poet to place them in this world and no other; but they admit of being placed there, Shakespeare resolved to place them there, and they lent themselves to his resolve. The resolve once taken to place the action in this world of problem, the problem became brightened by all the force of Shakespeare's faculties, of Shakespeare's subtlety. 'Hamlet' thus comes at last to be not a drama followed with perfect comprehension and profoundest emotion, which is the ideal for tragedy, but a problem soliciting interpretation and solution.

ANON.

DEVICE of man in working hath no end;
What thought can think, another thought can
mend.

SOUTHWELL.

If ever sat at any good man's feast—

AS YOU LIKE IT ii. 7.

JUST outside the town I came upon an old English cottage, or mansion, I hardly know which to call it, set close under the hill, and beside the river, perhaps built somewhere in the Charleses' times, with mullioned windows and a low-arched porch; round which, in the little triangular garden, one can imagine the family as they used to sit in old summer times, the ripple of the river heard faintly through the sweet-briar hedge, and the sheep on the far-off wolds shining in the evening sunlight.

RUSKIN.

WHAT neat repast shall feast us, light and choice,
Of Attic taste, with wine, whence we may rise
To hear the lute well touched, or artful voice
Warble immortal notes and Tuscan air?
He who of these delights can judge, and spare
To interpose them oft, is not unwise.

MILTON.

AUGUST 23

Base is the slave that pays.

KING HENRY V. ii. I.

'MY other piece of advice, Copperfield,' said Mr. Micawber, 'you know. Annual income twenty pounds, annual expenditure nineteen nineteen six, result happiness. Annual income twenty pounds, annual expenditure twenty pounds ought and six, result misery. The blossom is blighted, the leaf is withered, the God of Day goes down upon the dreary scene, and—in short you are for ever floored. As I am!'

DICKENS.

THERE 's one request I make to Him
  Who sits the clouds above:
That I were fairly out of debt,
  As I am out of love.

'Tis only being in love, or debt,
  That robs us of our rest,
And he that is quite out of both,
  Of all the world is blest.

SUCKLING.

Look whether he has not turned his colour and has tears in 's eyes. Pray you, no more.

HAMLET ii. 2.

MOREOVER pathos is a tide; often it carries the awakener of it off his feet, and whirls him over and over, armour and all, in ignominious attitudes of helpless prostration, whereof he may well be ashamed in the retrospect. We cannot quite preserve our dignity when we stoop to the work of calling forth tears. Moses had probably to take a nimble jump away from the rock, after that venerable law-giver had knocked the water out of it.

GEORGE MEREDITH.

—COULD face his soul so to his own conceit
That from her working all his visage warm'd,
Tears in his eyes, distraction in 's aspect,
A broken voice, and his whole function suiting
With forms to his conceit, and all for nothing!

HAMLET ii. 2.

AUGUST 25

If she be made of white and red,
Her faults will ne'er be known.

LOVE'S LABOUR'S LOST i. 2.

THE advantages of natural folly in a beautiful girl have been already set forth by the capital pen of a sister author; and to her treatment of the subject I will only add, in justice to men, that though to the larger and more trifling part of the sex, imbecility in females is a great enhancement of their personal charms, there is a portion of them too reasonable, and too well informed themselves, to desire anything more in woman than ignorance.

JANE AUSTEN.

Hath white and red in it such wondrous power
That it can pierce through the eyes into the heart?

SPENSER.

Bewitching like the wanton mermaid's songs,
Yet from mine ear the tempting tune is blown.

VENUS AND ADONIS.

THE ideal, cheerful, sensuous, Pagan life is not sick or sorry. No; yet its natural end is the sort of life which Pompeii and Herculaneum bring so vividly before us,—a life which by no means in itself suggests the thought of horror and misery, which even, in many ways, gratifies the senses and the understanding; but by the very intensity and unremittingness of its appeal to the senses and the understanding, by its stimulating a single side of us too absolutely, ends by fatiguing and revolting us; ends by leaving us with a sense of confinement, of oppression,—with a desire for an utter change, for clouds, storms, effusion, and relief.

MATTHEW ARNOLD.

I FLUNG away, and with full cry
Of wild affections, rid
In post for pleasures, bent to try
All gamesters that would bid.
I played with fire, did counsel spurn,
Made life my common stake;
But never thought that fire would burn,
Or that a soul could ache.

VAUGHAN.

These things seem small and undistinguishable,
Like far-off mountains turned into clouds.

MIDSUMMER-NIGHT'S DREAM IV. I.

WHEN we read over the siege of *Troy*, which lasted ten years and eight months,—though with such a train of artillery as we had at *Namur*, the town might have been carried in a week,—was I not as much concerned for the *Greeks* and *Trojans* as any boy of the whole school? Did any of you shed more tears for *Hector*? And when King *Priam* came to the camp to beg his body, and returned weeping back to *Troy* without it,—you know, brother, I could not eat my dinner.

STERNE.

WE travelled in the print of olden wars,
Yet all the land was green,
And love we found, and peace,
Where fire and war had been.

They pass and smile, the children of the sword—
No more the sword they wield,
And O, how deep the corn
Along the battlefield!

LOUIS STEVENSON.

What is that curt'sy worth? or those doves' eyes,
Which can make gods forsworn? I melt, and am not
Of stronger earth than others.

CORIOLANUS V. 3.

TO say the truth, perfect beauty in both sexes is a more irresistible object than it is generally thought; for, notwithstanding some of us are contented with more homely lots, and learn by rote (as children are apt to repeat what gives them no idea) to despise outside, and to value more solid charms; yet I have always observed, at the approach of consummate beauty, that these more solid charms only shine with that kind of lustre which the stars have after the rising of the sun.

FIELDING.

THINK not, it was those colours white and red
Laid but on flesh, that could affect me so,
But something else, which thought holds under lock
And hath no key of words to open it.
They are the smallest pieces of the mind
That pass this narrow organ of the voice.
The great remain behind in that vast orb
Of th' apprehension, and are never born.

DANIEL.

To o'erthrow law and in one self-born hour
To plant and o'erwhelm custom.

WINTER'S TALE iv. I.

IT is a sour, malignant, and envious disposition, without taste for the reality, and for any image or representation of virtue, that sees with joy the unmerited fall of what had long flourished in splendour and in honour. I do not like to see anything destroyed, any void produced in society, any ruin on the face of the land.

BURKE.

AND what if she had seen those glories fade,
Those titles vanish, and that strength decay,—
Yet shall some tribute of regret be paid
When her long life hath reach'd its final day;
Men are we, and must grieve when even the shade
Of that which once was great has pass'd away.

WORDSWORTH.

'Tis the times' plague, when madmen lead the blind.

KING LEAR iv. i.

I BEG leave to subscribe my assent to Mr. Burke's creed on the Revolution of France. I admire his eloquence, I approve his politics, I adore his chivalry, and I can almost excuse his reverence for church establishments. I have sometimes thought of writing a Dialogue of the Dead, in which Lucian, Erasmus, and Voltaire should mutually acknowledge the danger of exposing an old superstition to the contempt of the blind and fanatic multitude.

GIBBON.

O STORMY people, unsad and ever untrue,
Ay undiscreet, and changing as a vane,
Delighting ever in rumble that is new,
For like the moon ay waxë ye and wane,
Ay full of clapping, dear enough a Jane;
Your doom is false, your constance evil preveth,
A full great fool is he that on you 'leiveth.

CHAUCER.

AUGUST 31

Summer's green all girded up in sheaves.

SONN. XII.

IN a genial August noon, beneath a sweltering sky, death is almost problematic. At those times do such poor snakes as myself enjoy an immortality. Then we expand and burgeon. Then we are as strong again, as valiant again, as wise again, and a great deal taller.

CHARLES LAMB.

RATHER by swath or furrow, or where the path
Is walled with corn I am found, by trellised vine
Or olive led in banks or orchard trim :
I watch all toil and tilth, farm, field, and fold,
And taste the mortal joy ; since not in heaven
Among our easeful gods hath facile time
A touch so keen, to wake such love of life
As stirs the frail and careful being, who here,
The King of Sorrows, melancholy man,
Bows at his labour, but in heart erect
A god stands, nor for any gift of God
Would barter his immortal-hearted prime.

ROBERT BRIDGES.

SEPTEMBER

Shall I compare thee to a summer's day?
Thou art more lovely and more temperate.

SONN. XVIII.

SIR, it is in the intellectual world as in the physical world: we are told by natural philosophers that a body is at rest in the place that is fit for it; they who are content to live in the country, are *fit* for the country.

DR. JOHNSON.

WHERE are the songs of spring? ay, where are they?
Think not of them; thou hast thy music too,
When barréd clouds bloom the soft-dying day
And touch the stubble-plains with rosy hue;
Then in a wailful choir the small gnats mourn
Among the river-sallows, borne aloft,
Or sinking as the light wind lives or dies;
And full-grown lambs loud bleat from hilly bourn;
Hedge-crickets sing, and now with treble soft
The redbreast whistles from a garden-croft,
And gathering swallows twitter in the skies.

KEATS.

In faith, they are as true of heart as we.

TWELFTH NIGHT ii. 4.

I SAY that both male and female are cast in one same mould; instruction and custom excepted, there is no great difference between them. Plato calleth them both indifferently to the society of all studies, exercises, charges, and functions of war and peace in his commonwealth. And the philosopher Antisthenes took away all distinction between their virtue and ours. It is much more easy to accuse the one sex than to excuse the other.

FLORIO'S *Montaigne*.

So God in Eve did perfect man begun:
Till then in vain much of himself he had:
In Adam God created only one,
Eve and the world to come in Eve He made.
We are two halves: whiles each from other strays
Both barren are; joined, both their like can raise.

OVERBURY.

I'ld give bay Curtal and his furniture,
My mouth no more were broken than these boys',
And writ as little beard.

ALL'S WELL ii. 3.

MR. PHŒBUS liked Lothair. He liked youth, and good-looking youth; and youth that was intelligent and engaging and well-mannered. He also liked old men. But between fifty and seventy, he saw little to approve of in the dark sex. They had lost their good looks if they ever had any, their wits were on the wane, and they were invariably selfish. When they attained second childhood, the charm often returned. Age was frequently beautiful, wisdom appeared like an aftermath, and the heart which seemed dry and deadened suddenly put forth shoots of sympathy.

LORD BEACONSFIELD.

THAT age is best, which is the first,
  When youth and blood are warmer;
But, being spent, the worse and worst
  Times still succeed the former.

HERRICK.

Well, for your favour, sir, why give God thanks, and make no boast of it; and for your writing and reading, let that appear when there is no need of such vanity. MUCH ADO iii. 3.

PATIENCE is the chiefest fruit of study. A man that strives to make himself a different thing from other men by much reading gains this chiefest good, that in all fortunes, he hath something to entertain and comfort himself withal.

SELDEN.

To either India see the merchant fly,
Scar'd at the spectre of pale Poverty!
See him, with pains of body, pangs of soul,
Burn through the Tropic, freeze beneath the Pole:
Wilt thou do nothing for a nobler end,
Nothing, to make Philosophy thy friend?
To stop thy foolish views, thy long desires,
And ease thy heart of all that it admires?

POPE.

Whose action is no stronger than a flower.

SONN. LXV.

ALL art constantly aspires towards the condition of Music. For while in all other works of art it is possible to distinguish the matter from the form, and the understanding can always make this distinction, yet it is the constant effort of art to obliterate it. That the mere matter of a poem, for instance—its subject, its given incidents or situation; that the mere matter of a picture, the actual circumstances of an event, the actual topography of a landscape—should be nothing without the form, the spirit, of the handling; that this form, this mode of handling, should become an end in itself, should penetrate every part of the matter:—this is what all art constantly strives after, and achieves in different degrees.

WALTER PATER.

It ceased: yet still the sails made on
A pleasant noise till noon,
A noise like of a hidden brook
In the leafy month of June,
That to the sleeping woods all night
Singeth a quiet tune.

COLERIDGE.

SEPTEMBER 6

The words of Mercury are harsh after the songs of Apollo. You that way: we this way.

LOVE'S LABOUR'S LOST V. 2.

THE Man of science seeks truth as a remote and unknown benefactor; he cherishes it and loves it in his solitude: the Poet, singing a song in which all human beings join with him, rejoices in the presence of truth as our visible friend and hourly companion. Poetry is the breath and finer spirit of all knowledge: it is the impassioned expression which is on the countenance of all science.

WORDSWORTH.

THOSE gipsies, so your thoughts I scan,
Are less, the poet more, than man.
They feel not, though they move and see;
Deeper the poet feels, but he
Breathes, when he will, immortal air
Where Orpheus and where Homer are.

MATTHEW ARNOLD.

So service shall with steelèd sinews toil,
And labour shall refresh itself with hope.

KING HENRY V. ii. 2.

IT is good to have been young in youth, and, as years go on, to grow older. Many are already old before they are through their teens; but to travel deliberately through one's ages is to get the heart out of a liberal education. Times change, opinions vary to their opposite, and still this life appears a brave gymnasium, full of sea-bathing, and horse exercise, and bracing, manly virtues; and what can be more encouraging than to find the friend who was welcome at one age, still welcome at another?

LOUIS STEVENSON.

But his past life who without grief can see;
Who never thinks his end too near;
But says to Fame, Thou art mine heir;
That man extends life's natural brevity—
This is, this is the only way
To outlive Nestor in a day.

COWLEY.

But now my gracious numbers are decayed.
SONN. LXXIX.

AS to matter of style, I have this to say: The language of the age is never the language of poetry; except among the French, whose verse, where the thought does not support it, differs in nothing from prose. Our poetry, on the contrary, has a language peculiar to itself, to which almost every one that has written has added something. In truth, Shakespeare's language is one of his principal beauties; and he has no less advantage over your Addisons and Rowes in this, than in those other great excellences you mention. Every word in him is a picture. Pray put me the following lines into the tongue of our modern dramatics:—

'But I that am not shaped for sportive tricks,
Nor made to court an amorous looking-glass'—

and what follows. To me they appear untranslatable; and if this be the case, our language is greatly degenerated. GRAY.

THEN crushed by rules, and weakened as refined,
For years the power of tragedy declined:
From bard to bard the frigid caution crept,
Till Declamation roared, while Passion slept.
DR. JOHNSON.

If thou hast not sat as I do now,
Wearying thy hearer in thy mistress' praise,
Thou hast not loved.

AS YOU LIKE IT ii. 4.

THE passion of love generally appears to everybody but the man who feels it entirely disproportionate to the value of the object; and though love is pardoned in a certain age, because we know it is natural, having violently seized the imagination, yet it is always laughed at, because we cannot enter into it; and all serious and strong expressions of it appear ridiculous to a third person; and though a lover be good company to his mistress, he is so to nobody else.

ADAM SMITH.

SILLY boy! 'tis full moon yet, thy night as day
  shines clearly;
Had thy youth but wit to fear, thou couldst not
  love so dearly.
Shortly wilt thou mourn when all thy pleasures be
  bereavèd.
Little knows he how to love that never was deceivèd.

This is thy first maiden-flame that triumphs yet
  unstainèd,
All is artless now you speak, not one word is feignèd.
All is heaven that you behold, and all your thoughts
  are blessèd,
But no spring can want his fall, each Troilus hath
  his Cressid.

CAMPION.

Come, thou monarch of the vine,
Plumpy Bacchus, with pink eyne!

ANT. AND CLEOP. ii. 7.

PRECIPITOUS, with his reeling satyr rout about him, re-peopling and re-illuming suddenly the waste places, drunk with a new fury beyond the grape, Bacchus, born in fire, fire-like flings himself at the Cretan.

CHARLES LAMB.

AND as I sat, over the light blue hills
There came a noise of revellers: the rills
Into the wide stream came of purple hue—
'Twas Bacchus and his crew!
The earnest trumpet spake, and silver thrills
From kissing cymbals made a merry din—
'Twas Bacchus and his kin!
Like to a moving vintage down they came,
Crown'd with green leaves, and faces all on flame,
All madly dancing through the pleasant valley
To scare thee, Melancholy!

KEATS.

There's none
Can truly say he gives, if he receives.

TIMON i. 2.

YEA, of my own inclination I am more officious towards the deceased. They can no longer help themselves, but (as me seemeth) they require so much the more my aid; there is gratitude, and there appeareth she in her perfect lustre. A benefit is less richly assigned where retrogradation and reflexion is.

FLORIO's *Montaigne.*

ON some fond breast the parting soul relies,
Some pious drops the closing eye requires;
E'en from the tomb the voice of Nature cries,
E'en in our ashes live their wonted fires.

GRAY.

How chances mock,
And changes fill the cup of alteration
With divers liquors.

2 KING HENRY IV. iii. 1.

WE accept the past for the same reason that we accept the laws of the solar system, though, as Comte says, 'we can easily conceive them improved in certain respects.' The past, like the solar system, is beyond reach of modification at our hands, and we cannot help it. But it is surely the mere midsummer madness of philosophic complacency to think that we have come by the shortest and easiest of all imaginable routes to our present point in the march; to suppose that we have wasted nothing, lost nothing, cruelly destroyed nothing, on the road.

JOHN MORLEY.

THE Moving Finger writes; and having writ
Moves on: nor all your Piety nor Wit
Shall lure it back to cancel half a Line,
Nor all your Tears wash out a Word of it.

FITZGERALD's *Omar Khayyám.*

Ah, what sharp stings are in her mildest words!

ALL'S WELL ii. 3.

FOR the rest of his character and habits, they were marked, as far as Elinor could perceive, with no traits at all unusual to his sex and time of life. He was nice in his eating, uncertain in his hours, fond of his child, though affecting to slight it; and idled away the mornings at billiards, which ought to have been devoted to business.

JANE AUSTEN.

For, boy, however we do praise ourselves,
Our fancies are more giddy and infirm,
More longing, wavering, sooner lost and worn,
Than women's are.

TWELFTH NIGHT ii. 4.

O let not Virtue seek
Remuneration for the thing it was.

TROIL. AND CRESS. iii. 3.

PRAISE is the reflection of Virtue. But it is as the Glass or Body, which giveth the Reflection. If it be from the Common People, it is commonly False and Naught: And rather followeth Vain Persons than Virtuous: For the Common People understand not many Excellent Virtues: The Lowest Virtues draw Praise from them: The Middle Virtues work in them Astonishment, or Admiration; But of the Highest Virtues, they have no Sense or Perceiving at all. But Shows, and *Species Virtutibus Similes*, serve best with them.

BACON.

THE wages of sin is death: if the wages of virtue
be dust,
Would she have heart to endure for the life of
the worm and the fly?
She desires no isles of the blest, no quiet seats of
the just,
To rest in a golden grove, or to bask in a summer
sky:
Give her the wages of going on, and not to die.

TENNYSON.

O swear not by the moon, the inconstant moon,
That monthly changes in her circled orb.

ROMEO AND JULIET ii. 2.

HE that hath a handsome wife by other men is thought happy; 'tis a pleasure to look upon her, and be in her company; but the husband is cloyed with her. We are never content with what we have.

SELDEN.

TELL me more, are women true?
Yes, some are, and some as you.
Some are willing, some are strange,
Since you men first taught to change.
And till troth
Be in both,
All shall love to love anew.

FLETCHER.

Most friendship is feigning, most loving mere folly.

AS YOU LIKE IT ii. 7.

TO speak indifferently, there are such multitudes that abuse the names of love and friendship, and so very few that either understand or practise it in reality, that it may raise great doubts whether there is any such thing in the world or not, and such as do not find it in themselves will hardly believe 'tis anywhere. But it will easily be granted, that most people make haste to be miserable; that they put on their fetters as inconsiderately as a woodcock runs into a noose, and are carried by the weakest considerations imaginable to do a thing of the greatest consequence of anything that concerns this world.

DOROTHY OSBORNE.

My true love hath my heart, and I have his,
By just exchange one for the other given:
I hold his dear, and mine he cannot miss,
There never was a better bargain driven:
My true love hath my heart, and I have his.

PHILIP SIDNEY.

What hour is this? or morn or weary even?
Do I delight to die, or life desire?

VENUS AND ADONIS.

OUR powers owe much of their energy to our hopes. When success seems attainable, diligence is enhanced; but when it is admitted that the faculties are suppressed by a cross wind, or a cloudy sky, the day is given up without resistance, for who can contend with the course of nature?

DR. JOHNSON.

EARLY he rose, and looked with many a sigh
On the red light that filled the eastern sky;
Oft had he stood before, alert and gay,
To hail the glories of the new-born day;
But now dejected, languid, listless, low,
He saw the wind upon the water blow,
And the cold stream curled onward as the gale
From the pine-hill blew harshly down the dale;
Far to the left he saw the huts of men
Half hid in mist, that hung upon the fen;
Before him swallows, gathering for the sea,
Took their short flights, and twittered on the lea;
And near the bean-sheaf stood, the harvest done,
And slowly blackened in the sickly sun.

CRABBE.

God shield I should disturb devotion!

ROMEO AND JULIET IV. I.

BEFORE leaving the church, I lingered a long time near the door, for it seemed to me I should not soon again enjoy such a feast of chiaroscuro. The opposite end glowed with subdued colour; the middle portion was vague and brown, with two or three scattered worshippers looming through the dusk; and all the way down, the polished pavement, with its uneven slabs glittering dimly in the distracted light, seemed to me the most fascinating thing in the world. It is certainly desirable, if one takes the lower church of Saint Francis to represent the human heart, that one should find a few bright places in it. But if the general effect is gloomy, is the symbol less valid? For the contracted, passionate, prejudiced heart, let it stand!

HENRY JAMES.

I CANNOT walk the city's sultry streets,
But the wide porch invites to still retreats,
Where passion's thirst is calm'd, and care's
unthankful gloom.

There, on a foreign shore,
The homesick solitary finds a friend;
Thoughts, prison'd long for lack of speech, outpour
Their tears; and doubts in resignation end.

CARDINAL NEWMAN.

SEPTEMBER 19

Tush, none but minstrels like of sonneting.

LOVE'S LABOUR'S LOST iv. 3.

IF there may be any reasons against children's making Latin Themes at school, I have much more to say, and of more weight, against their making verses—verses of any sort. For if he has no genius to poetry, 'tis the most unreasonable thing in the world to torment a child and waste his time about that which can never succeed; and if he have a poetic vein, 'tis to me the strangest thing in the world that the father should desire or suffer it to be cherished or improved. Methinks the parents should labour to have it stifled and suppressed as much as may be; and I know not what reason a father can have to wish his son a poet, who does not desire to have him bid defiance to all other callings and business. LOCKE.

YEARS following years, steal something ev'ry day
At last they steal us from ourselves away;
In one our Frolics, one Amusements end,
In one a Mistress drops, in one a Friend;
This subtle Thief of life, this paltry Time,
What will it leave me, if it snatch my rhyme?
If ev'ry wheel of that unweary'd Mill,
Which turn'd ten thousand verses, now stand still?

POPE.

SEPTEMBER 20

I am the man! If it be so (as 'tis),
Poor lady, she were better love a dream.

TWELFTH NIGHT ii. 2.

YOU are right about 'Antigone'; how sublime a picture of a woman! and what think you of the choruses, and especially of the lyrical complaints of the godlike victim? and the menaces of Tiresias and their rapid fulfilment? Some of us have, in a prior existence, been in love with an Antigone, and that makes us find no full content in any mortal tie.

SHELLEY.

I FEAR thy kisses, gentle maiden,
Thou needest not fear mine;
My spirit is too deeply laden
Ever to burthen thine.

I fear thy mien, thy tones, thy motion,
Thou needest not fear mine;
Innocent is the heart's devotion
With which I worship thine.

SHELLEY.

For thee watch I whilst thou dost wake elsewhere,
From me far off, with others all too near.

SONN. LXI.

'SHE did not care,' she said to herself; as people say they do not care, when they know in their heart of hearts that they have but to speak to call a welcome answering voice, to put out their hand for another hand to grasp. They do not say so when all is really gone, and there is no answer anywhere.

MISS THACKERAY.

No answer through the moonlit night,
  No answer in the cold grey dawn,
  No answer when the shaven lawn
Grew green, and all the roses bright.

WILLIAM MORRIS.

Harm have I done to them, but ne'er was harm'd;
Kept hearts in liveries, but mine own was free.

A LOVER'S COMPLAINT.

NATURE had disposed her for coquetry, which is a pastime counting among the arts of fence, and often innocent, often serviceable, though sometimes dangerous, in the centres of polished barbarism known as aristocratic societies, where nature is not absent, but on the contrary very extravagant, tropical, by reason of her idle hours for the imbibing of copious draughts of sunlight.

GEORGE MEREDITH.

DORINDA'S sparkling wit and eyes
United, cast too fierce a light,
Which blazes high, but quickly dies;
Pains not the heart, but hurts the sight.

Love is a calmer, gentler joy:
Smooth are his looks, and soft his face;
Her Cupid is a blackguard boy,
That runs his link full in your face.

CH. SACKVILLE, EARL OF DORSET.

Thou bear'st thy heavy riches but a journey,
And death unloads thee.

MEASURE FOR MEASURE iii. I.

WHEN Goliah had armed and fortified this body, and Jezabel had painted and perfumed this body, and Dives had pampered and larded this body, as God said to Ezekiel, when he brought him to the dry bones, *Fili hominis,* Son of man, doest thou think these bones can live? They said in their hearts to all the world, can these bodies die? And they are dead. Jezabel's dust is not Amber, nor Goliah's dust *Terra Sigillata,* medicinal, nor does the Serpent, whose meat they are both, find any better relish in Dives than in Lazarus.

DONNE.

LET no man awe thee on any height
Of earthly kinship's mouldering night.
The dust his heel holds meet for thy brow
Hath all of it been what both are now;
And thou and he may plague together
A beggar's eyes in some dusty weather
When none that is now knows sound or sight.

D. G. ROSSETTI.

Or else misgraffed in respect of years—

MIDSUMMER-NIGHT'S DREAM i. I.

IN September I saw a tree bearing roses, whilst others of the same kind round about it were barren. Demanding the cause of the gardener why that tree was an exception from the rule of the rest, this reason was rendered ; because that alone being clipped close in May, was then hindered to spring and sprout, and therefore took this advantage by itself to bud in autumn.

FULLER.

WHY came I so untimely forth
Into a world which, wanting thee,
Could entertain us with no worth
Or shadow of felicity,
That time should me so far remove
From that which I was born to love?

WALLER.

Groves
Whose shadow the dismissed bachelor loves,
Being lass-lorn.

TEMPEST iv. 1.

HE told him a very true story of a gentleman who not long before had come for some time to lodge there, and found all the people he came in company with bewailing the death of a gentlewoman that had lived there. Hearing her so much deplored, he made inquiry after her, and grew so much in love with the description that no other discourse could at first please him, nor could he at last endure any other; he grew desperately melancholy, and would go to a mount where the print of her foot was cut, and lie there pining and kissing of it all the day long, till at length death, in some months' space, concluded his languishment.

MRS. HUTCHINSON.

THERE comes a murmur from the shore,
And in the place two fair streams are,
Drawn from the purple hills afar,
Drawn down unto the restless sea;
The hills whose flowers ne'er fed the bee,
The shore no ship has ever seen,
Still beaten by the billows green,
Whose murmur comes unceasingly
Unto the place for which I cry.

WILLIAM MORRIS.

Who doth ambition shun,
And loves to live i' the sun—

AS YOU LIKE IT ii. 5.

AND so you have a garden of your own, and you plant and transplant, and are dirty and amused! Are you not ashamed of yourself? Why, I have no such thing, you monster, nor ever shall be either dirty or amused as long as I live. My gardens are in the windows like those of a lodger up three pair of stairs in Petticoat Lane, or Camomile Street, and they go to bed regularly under the same roof that I do.

GRAY.

BUT well He knew what place would best agree
With innocence and with felicity;
And we elsewhere still seek for them in vain.
If any part of either yet remain,
If any part of either we expect,
This may our judgment in the search direct,
God the first garden made, and the first city, Cain.

COWLEY.

O, thou wilt be a wilderness again,
Peopled with wolves, thy old inhabitants!

2 KING HENRY IV. iv. 5.

WHEN London shall be an habitation of bitterns, when St. Paul's and Westminster Abbey shall stand, shapeless and nameless ruins, in the midst of an unpeopled marsh; when the piers of Waterloo Bridge shall become the nuclei of islets of reeds and osiers, and cast the jagged shadows of their broken arches on the solitary stream—

SHELLEY.

PURGED by the sword, and purified by fire,
  Then had we seen proud London's hated walls;
Owls would have hooted in St. Peter's choir,
  And foxes stunk and littered in St. Paul's.

GRAY.

When forty winters shall besiege thy brow.

SONN. II.

AN old, a grave discreet man, is fittest to discourse of love matters; because he hath likely more experience, observed more, hath a more staid judgment, can better discern, resolve, discuss, advise, give better cautions and more solid precepts, better inform his auditors in such a subject, and by reason of his riper years, sooner divert.

BURTON.

CURLY gold locks cover foolish brains,
  Billing and cooing is all your cheer;
Sighing and singing of midnight strains
Under Bonnybell's window panes—
  Wait till you come to forty year.

Forty times over let Michaelmas pass,
  Grizzling hair the brain doth clear—
Then you know a boy is an ass,
Then you know the worth of a lass,
  Once you have come to forty year.

THACKERAY.

Angels are bright still, though the brightest fell.

MACBETH iv. 3.

THE angel choirs of Angelico, with the flames on their white foreheads waving brighter as they move, and the sparkles streaming from their purple wings like the glitter of many suns upon a sounding sea, listening in the pauses of alternate song, for the prolonging of the trumpet-blast, and the answering of psaltery and cymbal, throughout the endless deep, and from all the star shores of heaven.

RUSKIN.

Ah! not the nectarous poppy lovers use,
Nor daily labour's dull, Lethæan spring,
Oblivion in lost Angels can infuse
Of the soiled glory, and the trailing wing.

MATTHEW ARNOLD.

My grief lies onward, and my joy behind.

SONN. L.

THESE walls surround green and level spaces of lawn, on which some elms have grown, and which are interspersed towards their skirts by masses of the fallen ruin, overtwined with the broad leaves of the creeping weeds. The blue sky canopies it, and is as the everlasting roof of these enormous halls.

SHELLEY.

WHEN Time is old, and hath forgot itself,
When water-drops have worn the stones of Troy,
And blind oblivion swallowed cities up,
And mighty states characterless are grated
To dusty nothing.

TROIL. AND CRESS. iii. 2.

OCTOBER

Like to the time o' the year between the extremes
Of hot and cold: he was nor sad nor merry.

ANT. AND CLEOP. i. 5.

DON QUIXOTE is of perennial interest, because he is the most powerful type ever set forth of the contrast between the ideal and the commonplace, and his figure comes before us wherever we are forced to meditate upon some of the most vital and melancholy truths about human life.

LESLIE STEPHEN.

SING some old rhyme of long ago
  Of lady-love and wandering knight,
Of faithful friend and valorous foe,
  And right not yet estranged from might.
The songs our singers sing us now,
O boy Comatas, sing not thou.

Sing, for thy voice has gentle power
  To cancel years of fret and woe,
And I remembering this one hour,
  Shall pass sad days the happier so,
And thou, before the sun has set,
O boy Comatas, wilt forget.

H. C. BEECHING.

Lovers' absent hours,
More tedious than the dial eight score times.

OTHELLO iii. 4.

ONCE more he turned, and his white handkerchief floated in the air. Molly waved hers high up, with eager longing that it should be seen. And then, he was gone! and Molly returned to her worsted-work, happy, glowing, sad, content, and thinking to herself how sweet is friendship!

MRS. GASKELL.

LET this sad interim like the ocean be
Which parts the shore, where two contracted new
Come daily to the banks, that when they see
Return of love, more blest may be the view;
Or call it winter, which being full of care
Makes summer's welcome thrice more wish'd, more rare.

SONN. LVI.

OCTOBER 3

O, no! the apprehension of the good
Gives but the greater feeling to the worse.

KING RICHARD II. i. 3.

PHYSICIANS are some of them so pleasing, and conformable to the Humour of the Patient, as they press not the true Cure of the Disease; and some other are so Regular, in proceeding according to Art, for the Disease, as they respect not sufficiently the Condition of the Patient. Take one of a Middle Temper; or if it may not be found in one Man, combine two of either sort.

BACON.

For what avails
Valour or strength, though matchless, quelled with
pain,
Which all subdues, and makes remiss the hand
Of mightiest? sense of pleasure we may well
Spare out of life perhaps, and not repine,
But live content, which is the calmest life:
But pain is perfect misery, the worst
Of evils, and excessive overturns
All patience.

MILTON.

OCTOBER 4

His garments are rich, but he wears them not handsomely.

WINTER'S TALE iv. 4.

MY tailor has brought me home a new coat, lapelled, with a velvet collar. He assures me that everybody wears velvet collars now. Some are born fashionable, some achieve fashion, and others, like your humble servant, have fashion thrust upon them. The rogue has been making inroads hitherto by modest degrees, foisting upon me an additional button, recommending gaiters; but to come upon me thus, in a full tide of luxury, neither becomes him as a tailor nor the ninth of a man.

CHARLES LAMB.

SOME glory in their birth, some in their skill,
Some in their wealth, some in their bodies' force,
Some in their garments, though new-fangled ill.

SONN. XCI.

OCTOBER 5

One touch of nature makes the whole world kin,
That all, with one consent, praise new-born gawds,
Though they are made and moulded of things past.

TROIL. AND CRESS. iii. 3.

THE component parts of dress are continually changing from great to little, from short to long; but the general form still remains; it is the same general dress, which is comparatively fixed, though on a very slender foundation; but it is on this which fashion must rest. He who invents with the most success, or dresses in the best taste, would probably, from the same sagacity employed to greater purposes, have discovered equal skill, or have formed the same correct taste, in the highest labours of art.

SIR JOSHUA REYNOLDS.

My love in her attire doth show her wit,
It doth so well become her:
For every season hath she dressings fit,
For winter, spring, and summer.
No beauty doth she miss
When all her robes are on,
But Beauty's self she is
When all her robes are gone.

ANON.

OCTOBER 6

Never war advance
His bleeding sword 'twixt England and fair France.

KING HENRY V. V. 2.

I CAN never mutiny so much against France, but I must needs look on Paris with a favourable eye: it hath my heart from my infancy. The more other fair and stately cities I have seen since, the more her beauty hath power and doth still usurpingly gain on my affection. I love that city for her own sake. . . . I love her so tenderly that even her spots, her blemishes, and her warts are dear unto me. I am no perfect Frenchman but by this great matchless city, great in people, great in regard of the felicity of her situation; but above all, great and incomparable in variety and diversity of commodities; the glory of France, and one of the noblest and chief ornaments of the world.

FLORIO'S *Montaigne*.

LET it not disgrace me,
If I demand, before this royal view,
What rub or what impediment there is,
Why that the naked, poor, and mangled Peace,
Dear nurse of arts, plenties and joyful births,
Should not in this best garden of the world,
Our fertile France, put up her lovely visage?
Alas! she hath from France too long been chased.

KING HENRY V. V. 2.

Comfort's in heaven; and we are on the earth,
Where nothing lives but crosses, cares, and grief.

KING RICHARD II. ii. 2.

'YOU are a philosopher, Dr. Johnson. I have tried, too, in my time to be a philosopher; but, I don't know how, cheerfulness was always breaking in.' Mr. Burke, Sir Joshua Reynolds, Mr. Courtenay, Mr. Malone, and, indeed, all the eminent men to whom I have mentioned this, have thought it an exquisite trait of character.

BOSWELL.

FADE far away, dissolve, and quite forget
What thou among the leaves hast never known,
The weariness, the fever, and the fret
Here, where men sit and hear each other groan;
Where palsy shakes a few sad last grey hairs,
Where youth grows pale, and spectre-thin, and dies;
Where but to think is to be full of sorrow
And leaden-eyed despairs;
Where beauty cannot keep her lustrous eyes,
Or new Love pine at them beyond to-morrow.

KEATS.

Well, honour is the subject of my story.
I cannot tell what you and other men
Think of this life.—

JULIUS CÆSAR i. 2.

THE martyr will not go to the stake in order that he may promote the happiness of mankind, but for the sake of the truth: neither will the soldier advance to the cannon's mouth merely because he believes military discipline to be for the good of mankind. It is better and safer for him to know that he will be disgraced if he runs away—he has no need to look beyond military honour, patriotism, 'England expects every man to do his duty.' These are to his mind far more definite motives than the greatest happiness of the greatest number.

JOWETT.

Poor, reckless, rude, low-born, untaught,
Bewildered, and alone,
A heart, with English instinct fraught,
He yet can call his own.
Ay, tear his body limb from limb,
Bring cord, or axe, or flame:
He only knows, that not through him
Shall England come to shame.

DOYLE.

OCTOBER 9

Wound me not with thine eye but with thy tongue.

SONN. CXXXIX.

WHAT is a difference? A word that means nothing,—a look a little to the right or to the left of an appealing glance. I think that people who quarrel are often as fond of one another as people who embrace. They speak a different language, that is all. Affection and agreement are things quite apart. To agree with the people you love is a blessing unspeakable. But people who differ may also be travelling along the same road on opposite sides.

MISS THACKERAY.

VIRTUE, how frail it is!
  Friendship, too rare!
Love, how it sells poor bliss
  For proud despair!

SHELLEY.

Youth no less becomes
The light and careless livery that it wears
Than settled age his sables and his weeds.

HAMLET iv. 7.

A GALLANT is one that was born and shaped for his clothes: and if *Adam* had not fallen, had lived to no purpose. He gratulates therefore the first sin, and fig-leaves that were an occasion for bravery. He is one never serious but with his tailor, when he is in conspiracy for the next device.

BISHOP EARLE.

THERE soon they chose
The fig-tree, not that kind for fruit renowned,
But such as at this day to Indians known
In Malabar or Deccan spreads her arms
Branching so broad and long, that in the ground
The bended twigs take root, and daughters grow
About the mother tree, a pillared shade
High overarched, and echoing walks between.

MILTON.

Farewell! thou art too dear for my possessing.

SONN. LXXXVII.

MAY my lady Dorothy suffer as much and have the like passion for this young lord, whom she has preferred to the rest of mankind, as others have had for her; and may his love, before the year go about, make her taste of the first curse imposed upon womankind, the pain of becoming a mother. May her firstborn be none of her own sex, nor so like her, but that he may resemble her lord as much as herself. May she, that always affected silence and retirement, have the house filled with the noise and number of her children, and hereafter of her grandchildren, and then may she arrive at that great curse, so much declined by fair ladies, old age; may she live to be very old, and yet seem young, be told so by her glass, and have no aches to inform her of the truth; and when she shall appear to be mortal, may her lord not mourn for her, but go hand in hand with her to that place, where we are told there is neither marrying nor giving in marriage, so that being there divorced, we may all have an equal interest in her again! WALLER.

LET us go hence, my songs; she will not hear.
Let us go hence together without fear;
Keep silence now, for singing-time is over,
And over all old things and all things dear.

SWINBURNE.

These earthly godfathers of heaven's lights,
That give a name to every fixed star,
Have no more profit of their shining nights,
Than those that walk, and wot not what they are.

LOVE'S LABOUR'S LOST i. I.

I HAVE never yet seen or heard anything serious that was not ridiculous. . . . All are to me but impostors in their various ways. Fame or interest is their object, and after all their parade, I think a ploughman who sows, reads his almanack, and believes that the stars are so many farthing candles created to prevent his falling into a ditch as he goes home at night, a wiser and more rational being, and I am sure an honester, than any of them.

HORACE WALPOLE.

It seemed far better to be born
To labour and the mattock-harden'd hand,
Than nursed at ease and brought to understand
A sad astrology, the boundless plan
That makes you tyrants in your iron skies,
Innumerable, pitiless, passionless eyes,
Cold fires, yet with power to burn and brand
His nothingness into man.

TENNYSON.

The love that follows us sometimes is our trouble,
Which still we thank as love.

MACBETH i. 6.

THIS family affection, how good and beautiful it is! Men and maids love, and after many years they may rise to this. It is the grand proof of the goodness in human nature, for it means that the more we see of each other, the more we find that is lovable. If you would cease to dislike a man, try to get nearer his heart.

J. M. BARRIE.

HARD is the doubt, and difficult to deem,
When all three kinds of love together meet,
And to dispart the heart with power extreme,
Whether shall weigh the balance down: to wit,
The dear affection unto kindred sweet,
Or raging fire of love to woman-kind,
Or zeal of friends, combined by virtues meet;
But of them all, the band of virtuous mind,
Methinks, the gentle heart shall most assurèd bind.

SPENSER.

Let determined things to destiny
Hold unbewail'd their way.

ANT. AND CLEOP. iii. 6.

SIBYLS and prophets have already spoken their inexorable decree, as Goethe has said, on the day that first gives the man to the world; no time and no might can break the stamped mould of his character; only as life wears on, do all its afore-shapen lines come into light. . . . The leaden chains of use bind many an ugly prisoner in the soul; and when the habit of their lives has been sundered, the most immaculate are capable of antics beyond prevision.

JOHN MORLEY.

By the hoof of the Wild Goat up-tossed
From the Cliff where She lay in the Sun,
Fell the Stone
To the Tarn where the daylight is lost;
So She fell from the light of the Sun,
And alone.

How the fall was ordained from the first,
With the Goat and the Cliff and the Tarn,
But the Stone
Knows only Her Life is accurst
As she sinks in the depths of the Tarn,
And alone.

RUDYARD KIPLING.

OCTOBER 15

Thou dost look
Like Patience, gazing on kings' graves, and smiling
Extremity out of act.

PERICLES V. I.

IT was at Rome, on the 15th of October 1764, as I sat musing amidst the ruins of the Capitol, while the bare-footed fryars were singing vespers in the temple of Jupiter, that the idea of writing the decline and fall of the city first started to my mind.

GIBBON.

Go thou to Rome,—at once the Paradise,
The Grave, the City, and the Wilderness:
And where its wrecks like shattered mountains
rise,
And flowering weeds, and fragrant copses dress
The bones of Desolation's nakedness,
Pass——

SHELLEY.

OCTOBER 16

It seems to me most strange that men should fear,
Seeing that death, a necessary end,
Will come when it will come.

JULIUS CÆSAR ii. 2.

BUT doctrines on this occasion, any other than that of living well, are the most insignificant and most empty of all the labours of men. None but a tragedian can die by rule, and wait till he discovers a plot, or says a fine thing on his *exit*. In real life, this is a Chimera; and by noble spirits it will be done decently, without the ostentation of it.

STEELE.

NOR love thy life, nor hate; but what thou liv'st
Live well; how long or short, permit to heaven.

MILTON.

OCTOBER 17

At the first sight
They have changed eyes.

TEMPEST ii. 1.

AND it appears to me, that in all cases of real love, it is at one moment that it takes place. That moment may have been prepared by previous esteem, admiration, or even affection—yet love seems to require a momentary act of volition, by which a tacit bond of devotion is imposed,—a bond not to be thereafter broken without violating what should be sacred in our nature.

COLERIDGE.

LOVE is enough: though the World be a-waning
And the woods have no voice but the voice of
complaining,
Though the sky be too dark for dim eyes to dis-
cover
The gold-cups and daisies fair blooming there-
under,
Though the hills be held shadows, and the sea a
dark wonder,
And this day draw a veil over all deeds passed over,
Yet their hands shall not tremble, their feet shall
not falter;
The void shall not weary, the fear shall not alter
These lips and these eyes of the loved and the
lover.

WILLIAM MORRIS.

The penalty of Adam,
The seasons' difference.

AS YOU LIKE IT ii. 1.

INDEED, by the report of our elders, this nervous preparation for old age is only trouble thrown away. We fall on guard, and after all it is only a friend who comes to meet us. After the sun is down and the west faded, the heavens begin to fill with shining stars.

LOUIS STEVENSON.

HE has his Summer, when luxuriously
Spring's honeyed cud of youthful thought he
loves
To ruminate, and by such dreaming high
Is nearest unto heaven: quiet coves
His soul has in its Autumn, when his wings
He furleth close: contented so to look
On mists in idleness—to let fair things
Pass by unheeded as a threshold brook.—

KEATS.

In me thou see'st the twilight of such day
As after sunset fadeth in the west.

SONN. LXXIII.

IN the evening I walked alone down to the lake by the side of Crow-park after sunset, and saw the solemn colouring of night draw on, the last gleam of sunshine fading away on the hill-tops, the deep serene of the waters, and the long shadows of the mountains thrown across them, till they nearly touched the hithermost shore. At a distance were heard the murmurs of many water-falls, not audible in the day-time; I wished for the moon, but she was *dark to me and silent,*

Hid in her vacant interlunar cave.

GRAY.

ANGELS and gods! *we* struggle with our fate,
While health, power, glory, pitiably decline,
Depressed and then extinguished: and our state
In this how different, lost star, from thine,
That no to-morrow shall our beams restore!

WORDSWORTH.

OCTOBER 20

When Love speaks, the voice of all the gods
Make heaven drowsy with the harmony.

LOVE'S LABOUR'S LOST iv. 3.

LOVE may spring in the bosom of a young girl, like Hesper in the evening sky, a grey speck in a field of grey, and not be seen or known, till surely as the circle advances the faint planet gathers fire, and, coming nearer earth, dilates, and will and must be seen and known.

GEORGE MEREDITH.

But the best is when I glide from out them,
Cross a step or two of dubious twilight,
Come out on the other side, the novel
Silent silver lights and darks undreamt of,
Where I hush and bless myself with silence.

BROWNING.

'Tis a kind of good deed to say well:
And yet words are no deeds.

KING HENRY VIII. iii. 2.

MR. COLERIDGE has a mind 'reflecting ages past': his voice is like the echo of the congregated roar of the 'dark backward and abysm' of thought. He who has seen a mouldering tower by the side of a crystal lake, hid by the mist, but glittering in the wave below, may conceive the dim, gleaming, uncertain intelligence of his eye: he who has marked the evening clouds uprolled (a world of vapours), has seen the picture of his mind, unearthly, unsubstantial, with gorgeous tints and ever-varying forms—

That which was now a house, even with a thought
The rock dislimns, and makes it indistinct
As water is in water.

HAZLITT.

So 'mid the ice of the far Northern sea
A star about the Arctic circle may
Than ours yield clearer light, yet that but shall
Serve at the frozen pilot's funeral.

HABINGTON.

Masters, remember that I am an ass; though it be not written down, yet forget not that I am an ass.

MUCH ADO iv. 2.

SIR WALTER ELLIOT, of Kellynch Hall, in Somersetshire, was a man who, for his own amusement, never took up any book but the Baronetage; there he found occupation for an idle hour, and consolation in a distressed one; there his faculties were roused into admiration and respect, by contemplating the limited remnants of the earliest patents; there any unwelcome sensation, arising from domestic affairs, changed naturally into pity and contempt, as he turned over the almost endless creations of the last century; and there, if every other leaf were powerless, he could read his own history with an interest that never failed. JANE AUSTEN.

That is honour's scorn,
Which challenges itself as honour's born
And is not like the sire: honours thrive,
When rather from our acts we them derive
Than our foregoers: the mere word 's a slave
Debosh'd on every tomb, on every grave
A lying trophy, and as oft is dumb
Where dust and damn'd oblivion is the tomb
Of honour'd bones indeed.

ALL'S WELL ii. 3.

Here are only numbers ratified; but, for the elegancy, facility, and golden cadence of poesy, caret.

LOVE'S LABOUR 'S LOST iv. 2.

POESY subsisteth by herself, and after one demeanour and continuance her beauty appeareth to all ages. In vain have some men of late, transformers of everything, consulted upon her reformation, and endeavoured to abstract her to metaphysical and scholastic quiddities, denuding her of her own habits, and those ornaments with which she hath amused the world some thousand years. Poesy is not a thing that is yet in the finding and search, or which may be otherwise found out.

DRUMMOND OF HAWTHORNDEN.

—Fair Nine, forsaking Poetry;

How have you left the ancient love
  That bards of old enjoyed in you!
The languid strings do scarcely move,
  The sound is forced, the notes are few!

BLAKE.

OCTOBER 24

There is a tide in the affairs of men,
Which, taken at the flood, leads on to fortune;
Omitted, all the voyage of their life
Is bound in shallows and in miseries.

JULIUS CÆSAR iv. 3.

THE race is not to the swift, nor the battle to the strong, neither yet bread to the wise, nor yet riches to men of understanding, nor yet favour to men of skill: but time and chance happeneth to them all.

ECCLESIASTES.

THERE is a deep nick in Time's restless wheel
For each man's good, when which nick comes, it strikes;
As Rhetoric yet works not persuasion,
But only is a mean to make it work:
So no man rises by his real merit
But when it cries clink in his Raiser's spirit.

CHAPMAN.

As easy might I from myself depart
As from my soul, which in thy breast doth lie.

SONN. CIX.

THEN they laughed and made good cheer, and either drank to other freely, and they thought never drink that ever they drank to other was so sweet nor so good. But by that their drink was in their bodies, they loved each other so well that never their love departed for weal neither for woe. And thus it happed the love first between Sir Tristram and La Belle Isoude, the which love never departed the days of their life. MALLORY.

No, no, fair heretic, it needs must be
But an ill love in me,
And worse for thee ;
For were it in my power
To love thee now this hour
More than I did the last ;
'Twould then so fall
I might not love at all ;
Love that can flow, and can admit increase,
Admits as well an ebb, and may grow less.

SUCKLING.

I gin to be aweary of the sun.

MACBETH V. 5.

I DO not envy the temper of Crows and Daws, nor the numerous and weary days of our Fathers before the Flood. If there be any truth in Astrology, I may outlive a Jubilee; as yet I have not lived thirty years, and yet, excepting one, have seen the Ashes, and left under ground all the Kings of Europe: have been contemporary to three Emperors, four Grand Signiors, and as many Popes: Methinks I have outlived myself, and begin to be weary of the Sun: I have shaken hands with delight in my warm blood and Canicular days; I perceive I do anticipate the vices of age; the world to me is but a dream or mock-show, and we all therein but Pantaloons and Antics, to my severer contemplation.

SIR THOMAS BROWNE.

THERE'S nothing serious in mortality:
All is but toys: renown and grace is dead;
The wine of life is drawn, and the mere lees
Is left this vault to brag of.

MACBETH ii. 3.

O, give me the spare men, and spare me the great ones.

2 KING HENRY IV. iii. 2.

WE mortals should chiefly like to talk to each other out of goodwill and fellowship, not for the sake of hearing revelations or being stimulated by witticisms; and I have usually found that it is the rather dull person who appears to be disgusted with his contemporaries because they are not always strikingly original, and to satisfy whom the party at a country house should have included the Prophet Isaiah, Plato, Francis Bacon, and Voltaire.

GEORGE ELIOT.

'TIS not in folly not to scorn a fool,
And scarce in human wisdom to do more.

YOUNG.

OCTOBER 28

Ay, by my faith, the field is honourable.

2 KING HENRY VI. iv. 2.

BEHOLD the original and primitive nobility of all those great persons who are too proud now not only to till the ground, but almost to tread upon it. We may talk what we please of lilies and lions rampant, and spread eagles in fields d'or or d'argent; but if heraldry were guided by reason, a plough in a field arable would be the most noble and ancient arms.

COWLEY.

THE Sword sang on the barren heath,
The Sickle in the fruitful field:
The Sword he sang a song of death,
But could not make the Sickle yield.

BLAKE.

Nor shall death brag thou wander'st in his shade,
When in eternal lines to time thou growest.

SONN. XVIII.

FOR to see things in their beauty is to see things in their truth, and Keats knew it. 'What the Imagination seizes on as Beauty must be Truth,' he says in prose; and in immortal verse he has said the same thing—

Beauty is truth, truth beauty,—that is all
Ye know on earth, and all ye need to know!

No, it is not all; but it is true, deeply true, and we have deep need to know it.

MATTHEW ARNOLD.

WHAT could the Muse herself that Orpheus bore,
The Muse herself for her enchanting son,
Whom universal nature did lament,
When by the rout that made the hideous roar
His gory visage down the stream was sent,
Down the swift Hebrus to the Lesbian Shore?

MILTON.

The prophetic soul
Of the wide world, dreaming on things to come.

SONN. CVII.

THE impression thus forced upon him connected itself with a feeling, the precise inverse of that, known to every one, which seems to say—*You have been just here, just thus, before!*—a feeling in his case not reminiscent but prescient, which passed over him many times afterwards, coming across certain people and places; as if he detected there the process of actual change to a wholly undreamed of and renewed condition of human body and soul.

WALTER PATER.

THRICE or thrice had I lov'd thee
Before I knew thy face or name.
So in a voice, so in a shapeless flame
Angels affect us oft, and worshipped be.

DONNE.

OCTOBER 31

Policy, that heretic,
Which works on leases of short-number'd hours.

SONN. CXXIV.

IT is not Juggling that is to be blamed, but much Juggling; for the World cannot be governed without it. All your Rhetoric, and all your Elenchs in Logick come within the compass of Juggling.

SELDEN.

Now, this no more dishonours you at all
Than to take in a town with gentle words
Which else would put you to your fortune and
The hazard of much blood.
I would dissemble with my nature where
My fortunes and my friends at stake required
I should do so in honour.

CORIOLANUS iii. 2.

NOVEMBER

'Tis set down so in heaven, but not in earth.

MEASURE FOR MEASURE ii. 4.

GOD'S calendar is more complete than man's best martyrologies; and their names are written in the book of life who on earth are wholly forgotten.

FULLER.

AND many more, whose names on earth are dark,
But whose transmitted effluence cannot die,
So long as fire outlives the parent spark,
Rose, robed in dazzling immortality.

SHELLEY.

My way of life
Is fall'n into the sere, the yellow leaf.

MACBETH V. 3.

ALL those arts, rarities, and inventions which vulgar minds gaze at, the ingenious pursue, and all admire, they are but the reliques of an Intellect defaced with Sin and Time. We admire it now, only as Antiquaries do a piece of old coin, for the stamp it once bore, and not for those vanished lineaments and disappearing draughts that remain upon it at present. And certainly that must needs have been very glorious whose decays are so admirable. He that is comely when old and decrepit, surely was very beautiful when he was young. An Aristotle was but the rubbish of an Adam, and Athens but the rudiments of Paradise.

SOUTH.

THAT time of year thou mayst in me behold
When yellow leaves, or none, or few, do hang
Upon those boughs which shake against the cold,
Bare ruin'd choirs, where late the sweet birds sang.

SONN. LXXIII.

Grief fills the room up of my absent child.

KING JOHN iii. 4.

WHICH of the dead are most tenderly and passionately deplored? Those who love the survivors the least, I believe. The death of a child occasions a passion of grief and frantic tears, such as your end, brother reader, will never inspire. The death of an infant which scarcely knew you, which a week's absence from you would have caused to forget you, will strike you down more than the loss of your closest friend, or your first-born son—a man grown like yourself, with children of his own. We may be harsh and stern with Judah and Simeon—our love and pity gush out for Benjamin, the little one.

THACKERAY.

A CHILD's a plaything for an hour;
  Its pretty tricks we try
For that or for a longer space,—
  Then tire and lay it by.

But I knew one that to itself
  All seasons could control,
That would have mock'd the sense of pain
  And of a grievèd soul.

MARY LAMB.

NOVEMBER 4

Have I not here the best cards for the game?

KING JOHN V. 2.

TO those puny objectors against cards, as nurturing the bad passions, she would retort, that man is a gaming animal. He must be always trying to get the better in something or other:—that this passion can scarcely be more safely expended than upon a game at cards: that cards are a temporary illusion; in truth, a mere drama; for we do but *play* at being mightily concerned, where a few idle shillings are at stake, yet, during the illusion, we *are* as mightily concerned as those whose stake is crowns and kingdoms. They are a sort of dream-fighting; much ado; great battling, and little bloodshed; mighty means for disproportioned ends: quite as diverting, and a great deal more innoxious, than many of those more serious *games* of life, which men play without esteeming them to be such.

CHARLES LAMB.

BEHOLD, four Kings in majesty rever'd,
With hoary whiskers and a forky beard;
And four fair Queens whose hands sustain a flow'r,
The expressive emblem of their softer pow'r;
Four Knaves in garbs succinct, a trusty band,
Caps on their heads, and halberts in their hand;
And parti-colour'd troops, a shining train,
Draw forth to combat on the velvet plain.

POPE.

For I am nothing if not critical.

OTHELLO ii. 1.

IT is undoubtedly true, though it may seem paradoxical; but in general, those who are habitually employed in finding and displaying faults are unqualified for the work of reformation; because their minds are not only unfurnished with patterns of the fair and good, but by habit they come to take no delight in the contemplation of those things.

BURKE.

I NEVER yet saw man,
How wise, how noble, young, how rarely featured,
But she would spell him backward: if fair-faced,
She would swear the gentleman should be her sister;
If black, why, nature, drawing of an antique,
Made a foul blot; if tall, a lance ill-headed;
If low, an agate very vilely cut;
If speaking, why, a vane blown with all winds;
If silent, why, a block moved with none.
So turns she every man the wrong side out
And never gives to truth and virtue that
Which simpleness and merit purchaseth.

MUCH ADO iii. 1.

O pretty Isabella, I am pale at my heart to see thine eyes so red: thou must be patient.

MEASURE FOR MEASURE iv. 3.

'WOMEN have two weapons,—rouge and tears,'—said Napoleon, as reported by Madame de Rémusat, who informs us that the Conqueror of Austerlitz was by no means proof against either implement. Lucky for mankind that the two are scarcely to be used with advantage at the same time.

PHILIP PRESTON.

Dear Chloe, how blubber'd is that pretty face!
  Thy cheek all on fire, and thy hair all uncurl'd:
Prythee quit this caprice; and, as old Falstaff says,
  Let us e'en talk a little like folks of this world.

How canst thou presume thou hast leave to destroy
  The beauties which Venus but lent to thy keeping?
Those looks were design'd to inspire love and joy:
  More ordinary eyes may serve people for weeping.

PRIOR.

NOVEMBER 7

Spirits are not finely touch'd
But to fine issues.

MEASURE FOR MEASURE i. 1.

IDEAS are often poor ghosts, our sun-filled eyes cannot discern them; they pass athwart us in thin vapour, and cannot make themselves felt. But sometimes they are made flesh; they breathe upon us with warm breath, they touch us with soft responsive hands, they look at us with sad sincere eyes, and speak to us in appealing tones,—they are clothed in a living soul with all its conflicts, its faith, and its love. Then their presence is a power.

GEORGE ELIOT.

LARGE was his soul; as large a soul as e'er
Submitted to inform a body here;
High as the place 'twas shortly in heaven to have,
But low and humble as his grave;
So high that all the virtues there did come
As to their chiefest seat
Conspicuous and great;
So low that for me too it made a room.

COWLEY.

NOVEMBER 8

Nay, if we talk of reason,
Let's shut our gates and sleep.

TROIL. AND CRESS. ii. 2.

DAUGHTER, daughter! don't call names; you are always abusing my pleasures, which is what no mortal will bear. Trash, lumber, sad stuff, are the titles you give my favourite amusement. If I called a white staff a stick of wood, a gold key gilded brass, and the ensigns of illustrious orders coloured strings, this may be philosophically true, but would be very ill received. We have all our playthings; happy are they that can be contented with those they can obtain.

LADY MARY WORTLEY MONTAGU.

Behold the child, by Nature's kindly law,
Pleas'd with a rattle, tickled with a straw:
Some livelier plaything gives his youth delight,
A little louder, but as empty quite:
Scarfs, garters, gold, amuse his riper stage,
And beads and pray'r-books are the toys of age:
Pleas'd with this bauble still, as that before;
Till tir'd he sleeps, and Life's poor play is o'er.

POPE.

Let's do it after the high Roman fashion.

ANT. AND CLEOP. iv. 15.

THE last year's papers had a bill of fare commencing with 'four hundred tureens of turtle, each containing five pints,' and concluding with the pine-apples and ices of the dessert. 'Fancy two thousand pints of turtle, my love,' I have often said to Mrs. Spec, 'in a vast silver tank, smoking fragrantly, with lovely green islands of calipash and calipee floating about—why, my dear, if it had been invented in the time of Vitellius he would have bathed in it!'

THACKERAY.

A TABLE richly spread in regal modes
With dishes piled and meats of noblest sort
And savour; beasts of chase, or fowl of game,
In pastry built, or from the spit, or boiled,
Gris-amber-steamed; all fish from sea or shore,
Freshet or purling brook, for which was drained
Pontus, and Lucrine bay, and Afric coast.
Alas, how simple, to these cates compared
Was that crude apple that diverted Eve!

MILTON.

Tell me thou lovest elsewhere, but in my sight,
Dear heart, forbear to glance thine eye aside!

SONN. CXXXIX.

I, THAT was wont to behold her riding like Alexander, hunting like Diana, walking like Venus, the gentle wind blowing her fair hair about her pure cheeks, like a nymph, sometime sitting in the shade like a goddess, sometime singing like an angel, sometime playing like Orpheus; behold the sorrow of this world! once amiss hath bereaved me of all.

RALEIGH.

For me (if there be such a thing as I!)
Fortune (if there be such a thing as she)
Finds that I bear so well her tyranny
That she thinks nothing else so fit for me.

And though she part us, to hear my oft prayers
For your increase, God is as nigh me here;
And to send you what I shall beg, his stairs
In length and ease are alike everywhere.

DONNE.

Her and her blind boy's scandal'd company
I have forsworn.

TEMPEST iv. 1.

SEEST thou not how Venus seeks to wrap thee in her labyrinth, wherein is pleasure at the entrance, but within, sorrows, cares, and discontent; she is a syren, stop thine ears at her melody; and a basilisk, shut thine eyes, and gaze not at her lest thou perish: . . . Daphne, that bonny wench, was not turned into a bay-tree, as the poets feign; but, for her chastity, her fame was immortal, resembling the laurel that is ever-green.

LODGE.

I ASK no kind return of love—
No tempting charm to please;
For from the heart these gifts remove
That sighs for peace and ease!

Nor peace, nor ease, the heart can know
That, like the needle true,
Turns at the touch of joy or woe,
But turning, trembles too.

MRS. GREVILLE.

Some there be that shadows kiss;
Such have but a shadow's bliss.

MERCHANT OF VENICE ii. 9.

THAT the end of life is not action, but contemplation — *being* as distinct from *doing* — a certain disposition of the mind, is, in some shape or other, the principle of all the higher morality. In poetry, in art, if you enter into their true spirit at all, you touch this principle, in a measure: these, by their very sterility, are a type of beholding for the mere joy of beholding.

WALTER PATER.

ARE they shadows that we see?
And can shadows pleasure give?
Pleasures only shadows be,
Cast by bodies we conceive,
And are made the things we deem
In those figures which they seem.

But these pleasures vanish fast
Which by shadows are exprest.
Pleasures are not if they last;
In their passage is their best:
Glory is most bright and gay
In a flash, and so away.

DANIEL.

I am myself indifferent honest; but yet I could accuse me of such things that it were better my mother had not borne me.

HAMLET iii. 1.

WHEN I religiously confess myself unto myself, I find the best good I have hath some vicious taint. And I fear that Plato in his purest virtue (I that am as sincere and loyal an esteemer thereof, and of the virtues of such a stamp, as any other can possibly be) if he had nearly listened unto it (and sure he listened very near) he would therein have heard some harsh tune of human mixture, but an obscure tune, and only sensible unto himself. Man all in all is but a botching and parti-coloured work.

FLORIO'S *Montaigne*.

But why to him confine the prayer,
When kindred thoughts and yearnings bear
On the frail heart the purest share
With all that live?
The best of what we do and are,
Just God, forgive!

WORDSWORTH

Exposing what is mortal and unsure
To all that fortune, death, and danger dare,
Even for an eggshell.

HAMLET IV. 4.

POOR soul, here for so little, cast among so many hardships, filled with desires so incommensurate and so inconsistent, savagely surrounded, savagely descended, immediately condemned to prey upon his fellow lives: who should have blamed him had he been of a piece with his destiny and a being merely barbarous? And we look and behold him instead filled with imperfect virtues.—

LOUIS STEVENSON.

O WEARISOME condition of humanity!
Born under one law, to another bound,
Vainly begot and yet forbidden vanity,
Created sick, commanded to be sound:
What meaneth nature by these diverse laws?
Passion and reason self-division cause.
Is it the mark or majesty of Power
To make offences that it may forgive?
Nature herself doth her own self deflower
To hate those errors she herself doth give—
For how should man think that he may not do
If nature did not fail and punish too?

LORD BROOKE.

What 's past and what 's to come is strew'd with husks
And formless ruin of oblivion.

TROIL. AND CRESS. iv. 5.

'THE greatest of painters only once painted a mysteriously divine child; he could not have told how he did it, and we can't tell why we feel it to be divine. I think there are stores laid up in our human nature that our understandings can make no complete inventory of. Certain strains of music affect me so strangely—I can never bear them without their changing my whole attitude of mind for a time, and if the effect would last, I might be capable of heroism.'

GEORGE ELIOT.

Is it that in some brighter sphere
We part from friends we meet with here?
Or do we see the Future pass
Over the Present's dusky glass?
Or what is it that makes us seem
To patch up fragments of a dream,
Part of which comes true, and part
Beats and trembles in the heart?

SHELLEY.

I have gone here and there,
And made myself a motley to the view.

SONN. CX.

'WHAT is your profession?' said Roberto. 'Truly, sir,' said he, 'I am a player.' 'A player!' quoth Roberto, 'I took you rather for a gentleman of great living, for if by outward habit men should be censured, I tell you, you would be taken for a substantial man.' 'So am I, where I dwell' (quoth the player), 'reputed able, at my proper cost, to build a windmill. What though the world once went hard with me, when I was fain to carry my playing fardel a foot-back; *Tempora mutantur*, I know you know the meaning of it better than I, but I thus construe it; it is otherwise now; for my very share in playing apparel will not be sold for two hundred pounds.' 'Truly' (said Roberto, 'it is strange that you should so prosper in that vain practice, for that it seems to me your voice is nothing gracious.' GREENE.

A STRUTTING player, whose conceit
Lies in his hamstring, and doth think it rich
To hear the wooden dialogue and sound
'Twixt his stretch'd footing and the scaffoldage.

TROIL. AND CRESS. i. 3.

It is but foolery; but it is such a kind of gain-giving, as would perhaps trouble a woman.

HAMLET V. 2.

AND mark Shakespeare's gentleness in touching the tender superstitions, the *terrae incognitae* of presentiments, in the human mind: and how sharp a line of distinction he commonly draws between these obscure forecastings of general experience in each individual, and the vulgar errors of mere tradition. Indeed, it may be taken once for all as the truth, that Shakespeare, in the absolute universality of his genius, always reverences whatever arises out of our moral nature; he never profanes his muse with a contemptuous reasoning away of the genuine and general, however unaccountable, feelings of mankind.

COLERIDGE.

You know that I held Epicurus strong
And his opinion: now I change my mind,
And partly credit things that do presage.

JULIUS CÆSAR V. I.

And like rich hangings in a homely house,
So was his will in his old feeble body.

2 KING HENRY VI. V. 3.

DIDST thou ever see a lark in a cage? Such is the soul in the body: this world is like her little turf of grass; and the heaven o'er our heads, like her looking-glass, only gives us a miserable knowledge of the compass of our prison.

WEBSTER.

RICHES I hold in light esteem,
  And Love I laugh to scorn;
And lust of fame was but a dream
  That vanished with the morn:

And if I pray, the only prayer
  That moves my lips for me
Is 'Leave the heart that now I bear,
  And give me liberty.'

EMILY BRONTË.

Who, all in one, one pleasing note do sing:
Whose speechless song, being many, seeming one,
Sings this to thee.—

SONN. VIII.

HIGH up around the Cupola runs a frieze of angels, singing together and dancing with joined hands, while bells composed of fruits and flowers hang down between them. Each angel is an individual shape of joy; the soul in each moves to its own deep melody, but the music made of all is one. Their raiment flutters, the bells chime; the chorus of their gladness falls like voices through a starlight heaven, half-heard in dreams and everlastingly remembered.

J. A. SYMONDS.

HEARD melodies are sweet, but those unheard
  Are sweeter; therefore, ye soft pipes, play on;
Not to the sensual ear, but more endeared,
  Pipe to the spirit ditties of no tone.

KEATS.

Men must endure
Their going hence, even as their coming hither:
Ripeness is all.

KING LEAR V. 2.

THE wood throws off its bark in large flakes, which one may find lying at its foot, pushed out, and at last pushed off, by that tranquil movement from beneath, which is too slow to be seen, but too powerful to be arrested. One finds them always, but one rarely sees them fall. So it is our youth drops from us,—scales off, sapless and lifeless—and lays bare the tender and immature fresh growth of old age. HOLMES.

SURE thou didst flourish once! and many Springs,
Many bright mornings, much dew, many showers,
Pass'd o'er thy head: many light hearts and wings,
Which now are dead, lodg'd in thy living bowers.

And still a new succession sings and flies;
Fresh groves grow up, and their green branches shoot
Towards the old and still enduring skies;
While the low violet thrives at their root.

But thou beneath the sad and heavy line
Of death dost waste all senseless, cold, and dark;
Where not so much as dreams of light may shine,
Nor any thought of greenness, leaf, or bark.

VAUGHAN.

For the time I study
Virtue, and that part of philosophy
Will I apply that treats of happiness
By virtue specially to be achieved.

TAMING OF THE SHREW i. 1.

LIKE the Scriptures, Plato admits of endless applications, if we allow for the difference of time and manners; and we lose the better half of him when we regard his Dialogues merely as literary compositions. Any ancient work which is worth reading has a practical and speculative, as well as a literary, interest. And in Plato, more than in any other Greek writer, the local and transitory is inextricably blended with what is spiritual and eternal.

JOWETT.

How charming is divine philosophy!
Not harsh and crabbed, as dull fools suppose;
But musical as is Apollo's lute,
And a perpetual feast of nectar'd sweets,
Where no crude surfeit reigns.

MILTON.

NOVEMBER 22

So, ere you find where light in darkness lies,
Your light grows dark by losing of your eyes.

LOVE'S LABOUR'S LOST i. 1.

ALL this is ours for the asking. All this we shall ask for if only it be our happy fortune o love for its own sake the beauty and the knowedge to be gathered from books. And if this be ur fortune, the world may be kind or unkind, it nay seem to us to be hastening on the wings of nlightenment and progress to an imminent millenium, or it may weigh us down with the sense of nsoluble difficulty and irremediable wrong; but vhatever else it be, so long as we have good health nd a good library, it can hardly be dull.

ARTHUR BALFOUR.

Myself, when young, did eagerly frequent
Doctor and Saint, and heard great argument
About it and about; but evermore
Came out by the same door where in I went.

With them the seed of Wisdom did I sow,
And with my own hand wrought to make it grow;
And this was all the harvest that I reap'd—
'I came like Water, and like Wind I go.'

FITZGERALD'S *Omar Khayyám.*

Stars, stars,
And all eyes else dead coals!

WINTER'S TALE V. I.

THE poor fellow who lost his arm last siege, will tell you, he feels the fingers that are buried in Flanders ache every cold morning at Chelsey.

STEELE.

WHAT needs complaints
When she a place
Has with the race
Of saints?
In endless mirth
She thinks not on
What's said or done
On earth:

She sees no tears,
Or any tone
Of thy deep groan
She hears:
Nor does she mind
Or think on 't now
That ever thou
Wast kind.

HERRICK.

Where virtue is, these are more virtuous.

OTHELLO iii. 3.

THERE is another mistake usual in mothers: if any of their daughters are beauties, they take great pains to persuade them that they are ugly, which the young woman never fails to believe springs from envy, and is perhaps not much in the wrong. I would, if possible, give them a just notion of their figure, and show them how far it is valuable. Every advantage has its price, and may be either over or under valued. It is the common doctrine of (what are called) good books, to inspire a contempt of beauty, riches, greatness, etc., which has done as much mischief among the young of our sex as an over desire of them.

LADY MARY WORTLEY MONTAGU.

It had been easy fighting in some plain,
  Where victory might hang in equal choice;
But all resistance against her is vain,
  Who has the advantage both of eyes and voice:
And all my forces needs must be undone,
She having gainèd both the wind and sun.

MARVELL.

To each of you one fair and virtuous mistress
Fall, when Love please! marry, to each, but one!

ALL'S WELL ii. 3.

HUMAN nature is so well disposed towards those who are in interesting situations, that a young person, who either marries or dies, is sure of being kindly spoken of.

JANE AUSTEN.

For either
He never shall find out fit mate, but such
As some misfortune brings him, or mistake;
Or whom he wishes most shall seldom gain
Through her perverseness, but shall see her gained
By a far worse; or if she love, withheld
By parents: or his happiest choice too late
Shall meet, already linked and wedlock-bound
To a fell adversary, his hate or shame.

MILTON.

Look! how a bright star shooteth from the sky.

VENUS AND ADONIS.

DEATH has not been suffered to take so much as an illusion from his heart. In the hot-fit of life, a-tiptoe on the highest point of being, he passes at a bound on to the other side. The noise of the mallet and chisel is scarcely quenched, the trumpets are hardly done blowing, when, trailing with him clouds of glory, this happy-starred, full-blooded spirit shoots into the spiritual land.

LOUIS STEVENSON.

AND him on whom at the end
Of toil and dolour untold
The gods have said that repose
At last should descend undisturbed—
Him you expect to behold
In an easy old age, in a happy home;
No end but this you praise.

But him on whom, in the prime
Of life, with vigour undimmed,
With unspent mind and a soul
Unworn, undebased, undecayed,
Mournfully grating, the gates
Of the city of death have for ever closed,
Him, I count *him*, well-starred.

MATTHEW ARNOLD.

To spoil antiquities of hammer'd steel,
And turn the giddy round of Fortune's wheel.

LUCRECE.

IN the Youth of a State, Arms do flourish: in the Middle Age of a State, Learning; and then both of them together for a time: in the Declining Age of a State, Mechanical Arts and Merchandise. But it is not good, to look too long, upon these turning Wheels of Vicissitude, lest we become Giddy.

BACON.

And so O leave to be
Sith thou art what thou art:
Let not our race possess
Th' inheritance of shame,
The fee of sin, that we
Have left them for their part:
The yoke of whose distress
Must still upbraid our blame,
Telling from whom it came.
Our weight of wantonness
Lies heavy on their heart,
Who never more shall see
The glory of that worth
They left, who brought us forth.

DANIEL.

Slanders, sir: for the satirical rogue says here that old men have grey beards, that their faces are wrinkled, their eyes purging thick amber and plum-tree gum, and that they have a plentiful lack of wit, together with most weak hams.

HAMLET ii. 2.

THIS fault, not to be able to know himself betimes, and not to feel the impuissance, and extreme alteration that age doth naturally bring, both to the body and the mind (which in my opinion is equal if the mind hath but one-half), hath lost the reputation of the most part of the greatest men of the world. I have in my days both seen and familiarly known some men of great authority, whom a man might easily discern, to be strangely fallen from that ancient sufficiency which I know by the reputation they had thereby attained unto in their best years.

FLORIO'S *Montaigne.*

UNFOLD thy flocks, and leave them to the fields,
To feed on hills, or dales, where likes them best,
Of what the summer or the springtime yields,
For love and time hath given thee leave to rest.

RALEIGH.

For, as thou urgest justice, be assured
Thou shalt have justice, more than thou desirest.

MERCHANT OF VENICE iv. I.

WHO shall put his finger on the work of justice, and say, 'It is there'? Justice is like the Kingdom of God—it is not without us as a fact, it is within us as a great yearning.

GEORGE ELIOT.

IF mercy be so large, where's justice' place?
—Where love despairs, and where God's promise
ends.
For mercy is the highest reach of wit,
A safety unto them that save with it:
Born out of God, and unto human eyes,
Like God, not seen, till fleshly passion dies.

LORD BROOKE.

The rest is silence.

HAMLET V. 2.

'HE was wild, sir,' Johnson said, speaking of Goldsmith to Boswell, with his great, wise benevolence and noble mercifulness of heart, 'Dr. Goldsmith was wild, sir; but he is so no more.' Ah, if we pity the good and weak man who suffers undeservedly, let us deal very gently with him from whom misery extorts not only tears, but shame; let us think humbly and charitably of the human nature that suffers so sadly and falls so low.

THACKERAY.

Sleep, and if life was bitter to thee, pardon,
If sweet, give thanks; thou hast no more to live;
And to give thanks is good, and to forgive.

SWINBURNE.

DECEMBER

When we shall hear
The rain and wind beat dark December.

CYMBELINE iii. 3.

THERE had been very little visiting; and though Miss Browning said that the absence of the temptations of society was very agreeable to cultivated minds, after the dissipations of the previous autumn, when there were parties every week to welcome Mr. Preston, yet Miss Phoebe let out in confidence that she and her sister had fallen into the habit of going to bed at nine o'clock, for they found cribbage night after night, from five o'clock till ten, rather too much of a good thing.

MRS. GASKELL.

Now winter nights enlarge
The number of their hours,
And clouds their storms discharge
Upon the airy towers.
Let now the chimneys blaze,
And cups o'erflow with wine;
Let well-tuned words amaze
With harmony divine.

CAMPION.

Every lane's end, every shop, church, session, hanging,
yields a careful man work.

WINTER'S TALE, iv. 4.

DO you know, after all, the meaning of this word *vulgar*? It is only common; nothing that is common, except wickedness, can deserve to be spoken of with contempt. When you have lived to my years, you will be disposed to agree with me in thanking God that nothing really worth having or caring about in this world is *uncommon.*

WALTER SCOTT.

Long have I loved what I behold,
The night that calms, the day that cheers;
The common growth of mother earth
Suffices me—her tears, her mirth,
Her humblest mirth and tears.

WORDSWORTH.

The Prince of Darkness is a gentleman.

KING LEAR iii. 4.

AN honest gentleman, and a courteous, and a kind, and a handsome, and, I warrant, a virtuous.

ROMEO AND JULIET ii. 5.

He above the rest
In shape and gesture proudly eminent
Stood like a tow'r ; his form had not yet lost
All her original brightness, nor appear'd
Less than archangel ruin'd, and th' excess
Of glory obscur'd : as when the sun new ris'n
Looks through the horizontal misty air
Shorn of his beams, or from behind the moon
In dim eclipse disastrous twilight sheds
On half the nations, and with fear of change
Perplexes monarchs. Darken'd so, yet shone
Above them all th' archangel ; but his face
Deep scars of thunder had intrencht, and care
Sat on his faded cheek.

MILTON.

'Tis not my profit that does lead mine honour;
Mine honour, it.

ANT. AND CLEOP. ii. 7.

I HOLD every man a debtor to his profession; from the which as men of course do seek to receive countenance and profit, so ought they of duty to endeavour themselves by way of amends to be a help and ornament thereunto.

BACON.

O, FOR my sake do you with Fortune chide,
The guilty goddess of my harmful deeds,
That did not better for my life provide
Than public means which public manners breeds.
Thence comes it that my name receives a brand,
And almost thence my nature is subdued
To what it works in, like the dyer's hand:
Pity me then, and wish I were renewed.

SONN. CXI.

Off, off, you lendings!

KING LEAR iii. 4.

AS I stood in the Mosque of St. Sophia, and looked upon these Four-and-Twenty Tailors, sewing and embroidering that rich Cloth, which the Sultan sends yearly for the Caaba of Mecca, I thought within myself: How many other Unholies has your Covering Art made holy, besides this Arabian Whinstone?

CARLYLE.

Go, tell the Court, it glows
  And shines like rotten wood;
Go, tell the Church, it shows
  What 's good, and doth no good:
If Church and Court reply,
Then give them both the lie.

RALEIGH.

To turn and wind a fiery Pegasus
And witch the world with noble horsemanship.

I KING HENRY IV. iv. I.

NAY, to such unbelieved a point he proceeded, as that no earthly thing bred such a wonder to a Prince, as to be a good horseman. Skill of government was but a Pedantry in comparison: then would he add certain praises, by telling what a peerless beast a horse was. The only serviceable courtier without flattery, the beast of most beauty, faithfulness, courage, and such more, that if I had not been a piece of a Logician before I came to him, I think he would have persuaded me to have wished myself a horse.

PHILIP SIDNEY.

WELL could he ride, and often men would say
'That horse his mettle from his rider takes:
Proud of subjection, noble by the sway,
What rounds, what bounds, what course, what stop he makes!'
And controversy hence a question takes,
Whether the horse by him became his deed,
Or he his manage by the well-doing steed.

A LOVER'S COMPLAINT.

Blind sight, dead life, poor mortal living ghost,
Woe's scene, world's shame, grave's due by life usurp'd.
KING RICHARD III. iv. 4.

BUT what are these to the instances, when we meet them, of the changes of our moral nature—to a life which grows poorer with its years—to the strange declensions of character, the chilling of enthusiasm, the quenching of love, the falls of the strong, the uncharitableness of the good, the failure of a great promise, the shaming of a great past? What are passing years, failing strength, and coming death to the sight of altering and dying goodness?

DEAN CHURCH.

ON parent knees, a naked new-born child,
Weeping thou satt'st while all around thee smiled;
So live, that sinking in thy last long sleep,
Calm thou mayst smile, while all around thee weep.

SIR WILLIAM JONES.

Men have died from time to time, and worms have eaten them, but not for love.

AS YOU LIKE IT IV. I.

HIS acquaintance with this high-born dame gave wit no opportunity of boasting its influence; she was not to be subdued by the powers of verse, but rejected his addresses, it is said, with disdain, and drove him away to solace his disappointment with Amoret or Phyllis. She married, in 1639, the Earl of Sunderland, who died at Newbury in the King's cause; and, in her old age, meeting somewhere with Waller, asked him when he would again write such verses upon her: 'When you are as young, Madam,' said he, 'and as handsome as you were then.'

DR. JOHNSTON.

YOUR shining eyes and golden hair,
Your lily-rosèd lips so fair;
Your various beauties which excel,
Men cannot choose but like them well:
Yet when for them they say they'll die,
Believe them not,—they do but lie.

ANON.

DECEMBER 9

My presence like a robe pontifical.

1 KING HENRY IV. iii. 2.

AND long it was not after, when I was confirmed in this opinion, that he, who would not be frustrate of his hope to write well hereafter in laudable things, ought himself to be a true poem, that is a composition and pattern of the best and honourablest things, not presuming to sing high praises of heroic men or famous cities, unless he have in himself the experience and the practice of all that which is praiseworthy.

MILTON.

THERE is a roaring in the bleak-grown pines
When Winter lifts his voice ; there is a noise
Among immortals when a God gives sign,
With hushing finger, how he means to load
His tongue with the full weight of utterless thought,
With thunder, and with music, and with pomp.

KEATS.

DECEMBER 10

The fann'd snow that's bolted
By the northern blasts twice o'er.

WINTER'S TALE iv. 4.

ALL the delicate poetry, together with all the delicate comfort of the frosty season, was in the leafless branches turned to silver, the furred dresses of the skaters, the warmth of the red-brick house-fronts under the gauze of white fog, the gleams of pale sunlight on the cuirasses of the mounted soldiers as they receded into the distance.

WALTER PATER.

I LOVE all that thou lovest
    Spirit of delight!
The fresh earth in new leaves drest
    And the starry night;
Autumn evening, and the morn
When the golden mists are born.

I love snow, and all the forms
    Of the radiant frost;
I love waves, and winds, and storms,
    Everything almost
Which is Nature's, and may be
Untainted by man's misery.

SHELLEY.

A sad tale's best for winter.

WINTER'S TALE ii. 1.

HE stood there amongst the Poor Brethren, uttering the responses to the psalm. The steps of this good man had been ordained hither by Heaven's decree: to this Almshouse! Here it was ordained that a life all love, and kindness, and honour, should end! I heard no more of prayers, and psalms, and sermon, after that. How dared I to be in a place of mark, and he, yonder among the poor? Oh, pardon, you noble soul! I ask forgiveness of you for being of a world that has so treated you—you my better, you the honest, and gentle, and good! I thought the service would never end, or the organist's voluntaries, or the preacher's homily.

THACKERAY.

His golden locks time hath to silver turned;
O time too swift! O swiftness never ceasing!
His youth 'gainst time and age hath ever spurned,
But spurned in vain; youth waneth by increasing.
Beauty, strength, youth, are flowers but fading seen;
Duty, faith, love, are roots, and ever green.

PEELE.

No man inveigh against the withered flower,
But chide rough winter that the flower hath killed.

LUCRECE.

I WISH beauty in her lost estate had consolations like genius. What needs them more? The reed is cut down, and seldom does the sickle wound the hand that cuts it. There it lies; trampled on, withered, and soon to be blown away.

LANDOR.

NE me ne list this sely woman chide
Further than the storië wol devise:
Her name, alas, is publishèd so wide,
That for her guilt it ought enough suffice:
And if I might excuse her anywise,
For she so sorry was for her untruth
I wis I would excuse her yet for ruth.

CHAUCER.

Life every man holds dear; but the brave man
Holds honour far more precious-dear than life.

TROIL. AND CRESS. V. 3.

GUILT and Shame (says the allegory) were at first companions, and in the beginning of their journey inseparably kept together. But their union was soon found to be disagreeable and inconvenient to both: Guilt gave Shame frequent uneasiness, and Shame often betrayed the secret conspiracies of Guilt. After long disagreement, therefore, they at length consented to part for ever. Guilt walked boldly forward alone, to overtake Fate, that went before in the shape of an executioner; but Shame, being naturally timorous, returned back to keep company with Virtue, which in the beginning of their journey they had left behind.

GOLDSMITH.

O MAN, strange composite of heaven and earth!
Majesty dwarfed to baseness! fragrant flower
Running to poisonous seed! and seeming worth
Cloaking corruption! weakness mastering power!
Who never art so near to crime and shame
As when thou hast achieved some deed of name.

CARDINAL NEWMAN.

Patience is sottish; and impatience does
Become a dog that's mad.

ANT. AND CLEOP. IV. 15.

IN those few days given us in the world, there is no man . . . that ever found himself so accompanied with happiness, but that he oftentimes pleased himself better with the desire and hope of death than of living, the incident calamities, diseases, and sorrows whereto mankind is subject, being so many and incurable that the shortest life doth often appear to us over-long,—to avoid all which there is neither refuge nor rest, but in death alone.

RALEIGH.

AND the dim low line before
Of a dark and distant shore
Still recedes, as ever still
Longing with divided will,
But no power to seek or shun,
He is ever drifted on
O'er the unreposing wave
To the haven of the grave.

SHELLEY.

Though thou the waters warp,
Thy sting is not so sharp
As friend remember'd not.

AS YOU LIKE IT ii. 7.

TO those that have been much together, everything heard, and everything seen, recalls some pleasure communicated, or some benefit conferred, some petty quarrel, or some slight endearment. Esteem of great powers, or amiable qualities newly discovered, may embroider a day or a week, but a friendship of twenty years is interwoven with the texture of life. A friend may be often found and lost, but an old friend can never be found, and nature has provided that he cannot easily be lost. DR. JOHNSON.

ALAS, they had been friends in youth;
But whispering tongues can poison truth;
And constancy lives in realms above;
And life is thorny; and youth is vain;
And to be wroth with one we love
Doth work like madness in the brain.

COLERIDGE.

DECEMBER 16

When icicles hang by the wall.

LOVE'S LABOUR'S LOST V. 2.

THE moon had just gone down, and the morning was pitchy-dark, and, as usual, piercingly cold. We soon entered the dismal wood, which I had already traversed, and through which we wended our way for some time, slowly and mournfully. Not a sound was to be heard save the trampling of the animals, not a breath of air moved the leafless branches. No animal stirred in the thickets, no bird, not even the owl, flew over our heads, all seemed desolate and dead, and, during my many and far wanderings, I never experienced a greater sensation of loneliness, and a greater desire for conversation and an exchange of ideas than then. GEORGE BORROW.

IN a drear-nighted December,
Too happy, happy tree,
Thy branches ne'er remember
Their green felicity;
The North cannot undo them
With a sleety whistle through them,
Nor frozen thawings glue them
From budding at the prime.

KEATS.

Now, the melancholy god protect thee; and the tailor make thy doublet of changeable taffeta, for thy mind is a very opal.

TWELFTH NIGHT ii. 4.

HE wastes the first half of a day in deciding which of two courses to take, and the second half in blaming himself for not having taken the other. He is constantly late at entertainments, because he cannot make up his mind in proper time whether to go or to stay at home; hesitation whether he shall read in the red room or the library, loses him three of the best hours of a morning; the difficulty of early rising he finds to consist less in rising early, than in satisfying himself that the practice is wholesome; his mind is torn for a whole fortnight in an absurd contest with himself, whether he ought to indulge a strong wish to exercise his horse before dinner.

JOHN MORLEY.

He who doubts from what he sees
Will ne'er believe, do what you please;
If the sun and the moon should doubt,
They'd immediately go out.

BLAKE.

I do not know what 'poetical' is: is it honest?

AS YOU LIKE IT iii. 3.

NOW, therein, of all sciences (I speak still of human) according to the human conceit, is our Poet the Monarch. For he doth not only show the way, but giveth so sweet a prospect into the way, as will entice any man to enter into it. Nay, he doth, as if your journey should lie through a fair vineyard, at the very first, give you a cluster of grapes, that, full of that taste, you may long to pass further. He beginneth not with obscure definitions, which must blur the margent with interpretations, and load the memory with doubtfulness; but he cometh to you with words set in delightful proportion, either accompanied with, or prepared for the well-enchanting skill of music, and with a tale, forsooth, he cometh unto you with a tale, which holdeth children from play, and old men from the chimney-corner.

PHILIP SIDNEY.

SYDNEIAN showers
Of sweet discourse, whose powers
Can crown old Winter's head with flowers.

CRASHAW.

Sap check'd with frost and lusty leaves quite gone,
Beauty o'ersnow'd and bareness everywhere!

SONN. V.

THE giant shadows sleeping amid the wan yellow light of the December morning, looked like wrecks and scattered ruins of the long, long night.

COLERIDGE.

A WIDOW bird sate mourning for her love
Upon a wintry bough;
The frozen wind crept on above,
The freezing stream below.

There was no leaf upon the forest bare,
No flower upon the ground,
And little motion in the air
Except the mill-wheel's sound.

SHELLEY.

For there was never yet fair woman but she made mouths in a glass. KING LEAR iii. 2.

HOWEVER, what has spoiled her for a mistress has improved her as a companion; and she is far more conversable now as she has much less beauty than when I used to see her once a week triumphing in the drawing-room. For, as few women (whatever they may pretend) will value themselves upon their minds while they can gain admirers by their persons, Timoclea never thought of charming by her wit till she had no chance of making conquests by her beauty.

MELMOTH.

COULD art, or time, or nature bribe
To make you look like beauty's queen,
And hold for ever at fifteen,
No bloom of youth can ever blind
The cracks and wrinkles of your mind:
All men of sense will pass your door
And crowd to Stella's at fourscore.

SWIFT.

We are such stuff
As dreams are made on.

TEMPEST iv. 1.

THE presence of a mystical element is the mark of all lofty imaginations. The greatest poet is he who feels most deeply and habitually that our 'little lives are rounded with a sleep'; that we are but atoms in the boundless abysses of space and time; that the phenomenal world is but a transitory veil, to be valued only as its contemplation arouses or disciplines our deepest emotions. Capacity for passing from the finite to the infinite, for interpreting the highest instincts before which our mortal nature

'Doth tremble like a guilty thing surprised,'

is the greatest endowment of the Shakespeares and Dantes.

LESLIE STEPHEN.

OUR birth is but a sleep and a forgetting:
The soul that rises with us, our life's star,
Hath had elsewhere its setting
And cometh from afar;
Not in entire forgetfulness
And not in utter nakedness
But trailing clouds of glory do we come
From God, who is our home.

WORDSWORTH.

Blow, blow, thou winter wind,
Thou art not so unkind—

AS YOU LIKE IT ii. 7.

'TIS a loss you are not here to partake of three weeks' frost, and eat gingerbread in a booth by a fire upon the Thames. Mrs. Floyd looked out with both her eyes, and we had one day's thaw: but she drew in her head, and it now freezes as hard as ever.

SWIFT.

April is in my mistress' face,
And July in her eyes hath place;
Within her bosom is September,
But in her heart a cold December.

ANON.

Like as the waves make towards the pebbled shore,
So do our minutes hasten to their end.

SONN. LX.

I WILL not argue the matter; Time wastes too fast, every letter I trace tells me with what rapidity Life follows my pen; the days and hours of it more precious,—my dear Jenny,—than the rubies about thy neck, are flying over our heads like light clouds of a windy day, never to return more; everything presses on,—whilst thou art twisting that lock; see! it grows grey! and every time I kiss thy hand to bid adieu, and every absence which follows it, are preludes to that eternal separation which we are shortly to make.

STERNE.

But at my back I always hear
Time's winged chariot hurrying near;
And yonder all before us lie
Deserts of vast eternity . . .
The grave's a fine and private place,
But none, I think, do there embrace.

MARVELL.

How shall your houseless heads and unfed sides,
Your loop'd and window'd raggedness, defend you
From seasons such as these?

KING LEAR iii. 4.

THE more carefully we examine the history of the past, the more reason shall we find to dissent from those who imagine that our age has been fruitful of new social evils. The truth is that the evils are, with scarcely an exception, old. That which is new is the intelligence which discerns, and the humanity which remedies, them.

MACAULAY.

Will poor folks lie,
That have afflictions on them, knowing 'tis
A punishment or trial? Yes; no wonder,
When rich ones scarce tell true. To lapse in fulness
Is sorer than to lie for need, and falsehood
Is worse in kings than beggars.

CYMBELINE iii. 6.

Wherein our Saviour's birth is celebrated.

HAMLET i. 1.

MY neighbour, or my servant, or my child, has done me an injury, and it is just that he should suffer an injury in return. Such is the doctrine which Jesus Christ summoned his whole resources of persuasion to oppose. 'Love your enemy, bless those that curse you': such, he says, is the practice of God, and such must ye imitate if ye would be the children of God.

SHELLEY.

SWIFT as the radiant shapes of sleep
  From one whose dreams are paradise,
Fly, when the fond wretch wakes to weep,
  And day peers forth with her blank eyes;
    So fleet, so faint, so fair,
    The Powers of earth and air
  Fled from the folding-star of Bethlehem.

SHELLEY.

But wherefore art not in thy shop to-day?
Why dost thou lead these men about the streets?

JULIUS CÆSAR i. 1.

ONE way of getting an idea of our fellow-countrymen's miseries is to go and look at their pleasures.

GEORGE ELIOT.

At morn and evening both
  You merry were and glad,
So little care of sleep or sloth
  These pretty ladies had;
When Tom came home from labour,
  Or Cis from milking rose,
Then merrily, merrily went their tabor
  And nimbly went their toes.

Witness these rings and roundelays
  Of theirs, which yet remain,
Were footed in Queen Mary's days
  On many a grassy plain;
But since of late Elizabeth,
  And, later, James came in,
They never danced on any heath
  As when the time hath been.

CORBET.

At Christmas I no more desire a rose
Than wish a snow in May's new-fangled mirth.

LOVE'S LABOUR'S LOST i. I.

ONLY in the city itself the winter was all the brighter for the contrast, among those who could pay for light and warmth. The habit-makers made a great sale of the spoil of all such furry creatures as had escaped wolves and eagles, for presents at the *Saturnalia*; and at no time had the winter roses from Carthage seemed more lustrously yellow and red.

WALTER PATER.

HOARY-HEADED frosts
Fall in the fresh lap of the crimson rose,
And on old Hiems' thin and icy crown
An odorous chaplet of sweet summer buds.
Is, as in mockery, set.

MIDSUMMER-NIGHT'S DREAM ii. I.

I cannot but remember such things were,
That were most precious to me.

MACBETH iv. 3.

I AT least hardly ever look at a bent old man or a wizened old woman, but I see also with my mind's eye that past of which they are the shrunken remnant; and the unfinished romance of rosy cheeks and bright eyes seems sometimes of feeble interest and significance, compared with that drama of hope and love which has long ago reached its catastrophe, and left the poor soul like a dim and dusty stage, with all its sweet garden-scenes and fair perspectives, overturned and thrust out of sight.

GEORGE ELIOT.

I STOPP'D and said with inly-muttered voice,
It doth not love the shower, nor seek the cold;
This neither is its courage or its choice,
But its necessity in being old.

WORDSWORTH.

Hang there like fruit, my soul,
Till the tree die!

CYMBELINE V. 5.

'AND then it went, "They that sow in tears shall reap in joy; and he that goeth forth and weepeth, shall doubtless come again with rejoicing, bringing his sheaves with him"; I looked up from the book, and saw you. I was not surprised when I saw you. I knew you would come, my dear, and I saw the gold sunshine round your head.'

She smiled an almost wild smile as she looked up at him. The moon was up by this time, glittering keen in the frosty sky. He could see for the first time now clearly, her sweet, careworn face.

'Do you know what day it is?' she continued. 'It is the 29th of December—it is your birthday! But last year we did not drink it—no, no. My Lord was cold, and my Harry was likely to die: and my brain was in a fever; and we had no wine. But now—now you are come again, bringing your sheaves with you, my dear.' She burst into a wild flood of weeping as she spoke; she laughed and sobbed on the young man's heart, crying out wildly, 'bringing your sheaves with you—your sheaves with you!' THACKERAY.

WITHIN the gentle heart Love shelters him
As birds within the green shade of the grove.
Before the gentle heart, in nature's scheme,
Love was not, nor the gentle heart ere Love.

D. G. ROSSETTI (*from the Italian of Guido Guinicelli*).

Welcome ever smiles,
And farewell goes out sighing.

TROIL. AND CRESS. iii. 3.

WHEN all is done, human life is at the greatest and the best but like a froward child, that must be played with and humoured a little to keep it quiet till it falls asleep, and then the care is over.

TEMPLE.

O WORLD! O life! O time!
On whose last steps I climb,
Trembling at that where I had stood before,—
When will return the glory of your prime?
No more—O never more!

Out of the day and night
A joy has taken flight;
Fresh Spring, and Summer, and Winter hoar,
Move my faint heart with grief, but with delight
No more—O never more!

SHELLEY.

The wheel is come full circle; I am here.

KING LEAR V. 3.

WE are now, reader, arrived at the last stage of our long journey. As we have, therefore, travelled together through so many pages, let us behave to one another like fellow-travellers in a stage-coach, who have passed several days in the company of each other; and who, notwithstanding any bickerings or little animosities which may have occurred on the road, generally make up all at last, and mount, for the last time, into their vehicle with cheerfulness and good-humour; since, after this one stage, it may possibly happen to us, as it commonly happens to them, never to meet more.

FIELDING.

Go thou forth, my book, though late
Yet be timely fortunate.
It may chance good-luck may send
Thee a kinsman or a friend,
That may harbour thee, when I
With my fates neglected lie.
If thou know'st not where to dwell,
See, the fire 's by.——Farewell!

HERRICK.

www.ingramcontent.com/pod-product-compliance
Lightning Source LLC
Chambersburg PA
CBHW032001120726
47898CB00005BA/1441

* 9 7 8 3 3 3 7 3 6 6 7 9 7 *